The Quest of the Fair Unknown

THE QUEST OF THE FAIR UNKNOWN

GERALD MORRIS

Houghton Mifflin Company
Boston 2006

For
Laura Crouch
Bill Mitchell
John D. W. Watts

Copyright © 2006 by Gerald Morris

www.houghtonmifflinbooks.com

The text of this book is set in 12.5-point Horley Old Style.

Library of Congress Cataloging-in-Publication Data
Morris, Gerald, 1963–
The quest of the Fair Unknown / by Gerald Morris.
p. cm.
Summary: Having grown up in an isolated forest, Beaufils sets off for Camelot
to find his father and winds up undertaking quests with Sirs Gawain and Galahad,
visiting various hermits, and traveling to the fairy world.
ISBN 0-618-63152-6
[1. Knights and knighthood—Fiction. 2. Adventure and adventurers—Fiction.
3. Identity—Fiction. 4. Gawain (Legendary character)—Fiction.
5. Galahad (Legendary character)—Fiction. 6. Humorous stories.] I. Title.
PZ7.M82785Que 2006   [Fic]—dc22   2005034850

ISBN-13: 978-0618-63152-0

Manufactured in the United States of America
MP 10 9 8 7 6 5 4 3 2 1

Contents

For this soul had to go forth to perform a deed so heroic and so rare—namely to become united with its Divine Beloved—and it had to leave its house, because the Beloved is not found save alone and without, in solitude.

—Dark Night of the Soul
Saint John of the Cross, 1542–1591

I

BEAUFILS

Beaufils gently laid his mother in the hole at the edge of the farmyard, then climbed out and sat in the grass. The day was warm, and digging the hole had been sweaty work. It was what his mother had said to do with her body after she died, though, so he didn't mind. After resting a moment, he stood, stretched his muscular arms and shoulders, and began filling in the hole with dirt.

She had also said that he should lay heavy stones over the soft dirt, and Beaufils—with the help of Clover the mule—had just finished dragging some rocks over to the hole and arranging them there when he saw the white-haired man at the edge of the clearing. Beaufils stopped in his tracks and stared at the man with wonder. In all his years in the forest, he had never seen any person besides his mother. This man wore a brown garment and was staring back at Beaufils with astonishment. It made Beaufils smile to think that he should be as amazing to the man as the man was to him, and that stir of amusement broke his trance. He said, "Hello, man."

"Good afternoon, lad," the man replied.

"It is, isn't it?" Beaufils said, raising his face to the sun. "But warm if you've been working. Clover and I need a drink. Would you like some water with us?"

"I would indeed," the man said. He stepped forward, and Beaufils led him to the well, where he dipped water for the mule first, then for the man, and finally for himself. When they had all had their fill, the old man looked at the mound of stones Beaufils had just left and said, "That looks like a grave, my boy."

"What's a grave?" Beaufils asked.

"A . . . a grave. A hole where you put someone's body after he dies."

"Is that what it's called?" Beaufils asked, interested. "I didn't know. Yes, that's what it is."

"May I ask who is buried there?"

"My mother," Beaufils explained.

The man's lined face grew grave. "I'm sorry, my boy. When did she die?"

Beaufils didn't understand why the man had apologized, since he had not caused her death, but he only

2

said, "Last night. I found her dead on her bed this morning."

The man stared at Beaufils. Then, in a sterner voice than he had used before, he said, "Your mother died only last night, yet you show no grief?"

"Mother said I wasn't to feel sad for her," Beaufils explained, "because she would be happier after she died, in a better place. She wasn't happy here these past months, I think. Her sickness made her hurt." He sighed softly. "I'm glad she doesn't hurt anymore, but I think I'll be sad sometimes anyway. It will be different without her."

"I see," the man said slowly, his voice gentle again. "You're right: Death is not sad for your mother. Her spirit is well now." Then, glancing curiously at Beaufils, he asked, "Forgive me, but if you didn't know what a grave was . . . Do you . . . do you know what I mean by 'spirit'?"

Beaufils nodded. "That's the part of you that knows things that the rest of you doesn't know."

The man looked struck by this. "Is that what your mother told you?"

"Oh, no," Beaufils said. "I figured that out on my own. Mother only told me what name to call it."

The man looked silently at Beaufils for a moment, then turned his head and examined the little house and shed and garden in the forest clearing. While the man looked around, Beaufils admired his brown garment. It was of cloth, like his mother's old dress, and it looked much warmer than Beaufils's own rough, sleeveless deerskin shirt. "Do you live here?" the man asked at last.

"Yes."

"For how long?"

"Always," Beaufils replied. "My mother came to this forest when she knew she was to have a baby. I was born in this clearing."

"Just you and your mother in this forest?" the man exclaimed, startled. "I thought these woods were uninhabited. But you must be seventeen years old!"

Beaufils cocked his head and considered this. The man evidently meant how many years it had been since he had been born, and never having thought about it before, Beaufils had to count back through the summers he had known. "Something like that, I suppose," he said at length. "But I'm not sure. I don't remember all the years when I was little."

"Amazing," the man said. "So long in this wilderness. Have you ever even seen another human?"

"No," Beaufils said. "You're my second, after Mother. But she told me there were others, so I wasn't *too* surprised to see you. Mother said that in some places there are *many* people."

"Yes," the man said in a dazed voice. "There are."

"Please, man," Beaufils said. "I don't know what she

meant by 'many.' In these other places, are there more than twenty people?"

"More than . . . ? Yes, there are more than twenty people."

Beaufils sighed. "That will make it harder."

"Make what harder, my boy?"

"Finding my father," Beaufils explained. "You see, when Mother knew she was soon to die, she told me to put her body in a deep hole—which seems very odd, but I suppose she knew best—and then said that I should leave our home to find my father."

"What is your father's name?" the man asked.

"Father, I suppose," Beaufils said. "That's what he is, isn't he?"

"Your mother didn't tell you another name? John? Rufus? William? Ambrosius Aurelius? Rumpelstiltskin?" Smiling with wonder, the man shook his head.

"No," Beaufils replied. "Do you mean that the people in those other places have special names like that?"

The man nodded. "Didn't your mother have a name?"

"Oh, yes," Beaufils said. "I called her—"

The man said it with him: "Mother."

Beaufils smiled. "That's right."

"And what did she call you?"

"Beaufils."

5

The man frowned briefly, *"Bo-feece,"* he repeated. Then his brow cleared. "Oh, I see. It's French. 'Fair son.' Of course." He sighed to himself. "You know, my boy, it might be harder than you think to find your father. Didn't your mother tell you anything about him?"

"Yes," Beaufils said. "She told me that he was a knight in a place called Camelot." The man's mouth opened, and he stared at Beaufils. "Please, man," Beaufils said, "what's a knight?"

Beaufils set off the next morning, despite his first friend's attempts to dissuade him from going. "You will be disappointed in the world beyond your forest," the man had said earnestly. "It is a bad place, filled with wickedness."

"What do you mean by 'wickedness'?" Beaufils asked. His mother had sometimes used the word when he was younger, when rebuking him, but he had not heard it in years.

Shaking his head slowly, the man said, "You don't even know, do you?"

"Well, I *think* I do," Beaufils replied. "It means doing things that your mother says you shouldn't do, doesn't it?"

"Yes," the man admitted. "I suppose so."

"Like picking scabs?"

The man closed his eyes. "I beg you, Beaufils, not to

go. Here, in this enchanted place, you are all unspoiled. It grieves me to think about the evil you will meet in the world."

Beaufils wasn't sure why the man was so worried; he knew better than to pick scabs now. He didn't want to argue, though, so he simply said, "My mother told me that people were not meant to be alone, and that once she was gone I should go find others like me."

"There *is* no one else like you," the man said.

"But there must be," Beaufils said. "One of them is my father. And besides, I have enjoyed talking to you very much; why should I not enjoy talking with other men as well?"

And so it was that Beaufils gave his forest cottage to the white-haired man—who seemed very pleased at the prospect of living there, hidden from the world—and started off the next morning on the back of Clover the mule. He rode southwest, which the man said was the way to Camelot, whistling bird songs to himself as he traveled. He took two pouches with him: one containing some vegetables and nuts to eat and the other filled with water. Before noon he had gone farther from his home than he had ever been, and everything he saw was new and exciting. There seemed to be treasures everywhere, and while he couldn't take every new wonder with him, by that evening he had already picked several fine keepsakes—a perfect swallow's nest, a white feather as long as his forearm, and a shiny black stone that had been polished smooth by a river. Beaufils couldn't imagine ever wanting more. He was enjoying his travels very much.

He set off the next day at sunrise, as soon as he and Clover had both eaten and had a roll in the grass. They continued traveling southwest, but Beaufils began to wonder how long it would take. Just how large *was* the world beyond? How far away was Camelot? For that matter, how would he know it when he arrived? All he knew was that there were knights there, but when he had asked the man about knights, his explanation had seemed so peculiar that Beaufils had concluded the man probably didn't really understand them himself. It was inconceivable to Beaufils that anyone would purposely wear such hard, heavy clothing as the man had said knights wore, and as for what knights did with those long poles—lances, the man had called them—well, that made no sense at all. Beaufils had politely refrained from asking any more questions about knights. He would just have to wait until he met someone else who was better informed. After all, the white-haired man was only the second person Beaufils had ever spoken with; he couldn't expect him to know everything.

He met his third and fourth humans around mid-morning. He was walking beside Clover across a grassy plain, giving the mule a rest, when two men with heavy black beards and very dirty clothes jumped out of a spinney and stood in front of him. They both carried thick sticks above their heads. "Stand!" one of them shouted.

Beaufils smiled a greeting and stopped walking.

"Hand them over!" the same man said loudly.

"What?" Beaufils asked.

"Your valuables," the second man said sharply.

Beaufils drew the nest, the feather, and the stone from his pouch. "You mean these?"

The two men looked at each other, and then, with loud, angry shouts rushed toward him. The nearest one was swinging his stick, and Beaufils saw at once that if he didn't move his head the stick would hit him, so he ducked enough to let the stick pass by. The man stumbled past and fell down. Then the other man swung his stick, and Beaufils had to step out of the way of this swing as well. For some reason, these men were actually trying to hit him with their sticks, which would hurt. Beaufils didn't want to be hit, so when the first man scrambled to his feet and swung at him again, Beaufils caught the stick as it went by and pulled it from the man's grip. Then, when the other man swung, Beaufils used it to deflect the blow. The second man struck three more times, and each time Beaufils tapped the blow away with his borrowed stick.

The attackers paused for a moment and backed off

a couple of steps. "Why are you trying to hit me?" Beaufils asked.

The two men looked at each other. "Something's not right here," said the one whose stick Beaufils had taken. "This boy ain't scared."

"Ay," replied the other one. "First he mocks us with birds' nests and rubbish, then he takes your cudgel away like you was a baby and fights me like a knight."

"Leave him be," the first one said. "We've had two good robberies in a row and we've got plenty of swag, even after splitting it between us."

Then, as Beaufils watched with amazement, the man who still had a stick drew back his arm and bashed the other man in the back of the head. The stricken man fell forward, and at once the other man pulled a pouch from his companion's belt. "Even more if we doesn't split it, see?" he said. Then he turned and ran away over the plain, leaving the first man face-down in the dust at Beaufils's feet.

"Are you all right, boy?" called a new voice from some distance off. Beaufils looked up to see two men riding huge animals, larger than Clover, approaching rapidly across the plain. Beaufils could only stare. The men wore the oddest clothing he had ever seen, clothing that shone in the morning sun, and each wore a hat that covered nearly his whole head, but for an opening in front. Beaufils realized that these were the knight's outfits that his friend had described, and he smiled with delight. So people really *did* wear such ridiculous garments.

"Are you knights?" he asked, smiling broadly at the two men as they approached.

"Ay, lad, that we are," said the knight who had called out earlier. "I'm Sir Bors, and this is my brother, Sir Lionel. Are you hurt?"

"No," Beaufils said. "But it's kind of you to ask. Are you?"

"These bandits are growing brazen, attacking boys in broad daylight," Sir Bors said. "I'll wager you gave them a bit of a shock, though. I saw the whole thing from that hill over there, and I've never seen neater work. Who taught you to fight, boy?"

Most of this was incomprehensible to Beaufils, but he had other things on his mind anyway. "What beautiful animals!" he exclaimed, reaching out to caress the face of Sir Bors's beast as soon as it was near enough. "What strength! Pray tell me, is this a horse?"

Sir Bors gaped at Beaufils briefly before replying. "Ay. This is a horse. Have you not seen one before?"

Beaufils shook his head, still beaming at the animals. "My mother told me about them, but they're far more magnificent than I'd imagined."

The other knight, the one called Sir Lionel, swung easily from his horse's back and knelt over the prone form of the fallen man, who was beginning to groan softly. Sir Lionel took hold of the man's leather garment at the back of the neck, then jerked him roughly to his feet. "Thought you had easy pickings, didn't you?" Sir Lionel said roughly. The man only groaned louder and put his hands on the back of his head. "And justly served for your infamy, you were. Still feel like making a living by thievery? How'd you like to rob me, hey?" Sir Lionel released the man, who sank immediately to his knees and began whimpering. "Oh, stop groveling, you cur," Sir Lionel said, pushing the man roughly back to the ground.

"Why are you shoving that man?" Beaufils asked.

"Eh?" Sir Lionel said, casting a curious glance at Beaufils. "Didn't he just try to hit you?"

"Yes, he did," Beaufils said. "I didn't understand that either."

"The fellow's a bandit," Sir Lionel said. "He meant to take your mule and everything else you have and probably leave you dead."

"He meant to do all that?" Beaufils asked, astonished. He thought of what the man in the forest had said about wickedness in the world. "I see," he said thoughtfully. "That's worse than picking scabs, isn't it?"

Sir Lionel chuckled, and Sir Bors said, "Ay, it is. But the lad's right, Lionel. The fellow's received justice. What he thought to do to the boy has been done to him.

No need to knock him about any more." Sir Bors turned back to Beaufils. "But you haven't answered my question: Who taught you to fight?"

"What do you mean?"

"The way you defended yourself with that cudgel. You'd make quite a swordsman, I'd say."

"You mean knocking away the other fellow's stick—cudgel, you say? Nobody taught me how; it just seemed the right thing to do."

"And so it was," Sir Lionel said, his eyes bright with laughter. He examined Beaufils appreciatively. "You're a likely looking lad. Good arms and shoulders. Judging from your leather jerkin, I'd say you were a woodsman."

Beaufils had never heard the term, but he liked it. "Yes, I suppose I am."

"I didn't know anyone lived off this way. Wild land, for the most part," Sir Lionel commented.

This didn't seem to require an answer, so Beaufils asked a question of his own. "Do you know the way to a place called Camelot?"

The two knights glanced at each other, then nodded. "Ay, lad," Sir Bors said. "We're from there ourselves. Are you going to Camelot?"

Beaufils smiled with pleasure. How simple everything had turned out to be. "You're knights from Camelot?" he asked, beaming.

"Yes."

"Then is one of you my father?"

The two knights looked at each other for a long moment. Sir Lionel's eyes were wary, and Sir Bors looked very solemn. At last Sir Lionel said, "Not that we know of, lad. Is . . . your father a knight from Camelot?"

Beaufils nodded, and Sir Bors said, "Ride with us, boy, and tell us the story."

Pleased with the invitation, Beaufils leaped onto Clover's back, pausing only long enough to glance at the still-groaning bandit and ask, "Should I give this man his cudgel back?"

"No," the two knights said in unison. Then they were off. It didn't take Beaufils long to tell about his mother and her instructions for him to find his father at Camelot, and when he was done, both knights were silent for a while. Sir Bors was frowning heavily, but Sir Lionel looked amused.

"Tell me this, boy," Sir Lionel asked. "If you do find your father, what do you mean to do with him?"

"Do with him?"

"To speak plain, do you mean to punish him?"

"Why would I do that?"

"For leaving your mother to raise you all alone, of course."

Beaufils puzzled over this. He had lived in the forest among the creatures long enough to know how these matters usually worked, so Sir Lionel's question took him by surprise. "Should he not have done so?" he asked.

"No," Sir Bors said emphatically. "He should not! It was the deed of a coward."

"But why?" Beaufils asked. "A stag mounts a doe and leaves her with young, then goes away. The doe raises the fawns, not the stag. Is that not how people do it?"

Sir Lionel shouted with laughter. "A lad after my own heart! Faith, I like this boy's attitude!"

"Be still, Lionel," Sir Bors said sharply. "You are betraying your morals!"

"And so are you, my gloomy brother, I assure you," replied Sir Lionel with a grin. "Why are you so offended? Has the boy not spoken the truth?"

"We are not beasts; we are men," Sir Bors snapped. "We live by a higher law." He turned to Beaufils. "How old are you, son?"

Remembering his talk with the man in the forest, Beaufils replied dutifully, "Seventeen, maybe?"

Sir Bors frowned again, even more severely, and muttered, "It could be. It could be."

"Oh, for God's sake, brother," Sir Lionel said, rolling his eyes. "Maybe you were right all along and should have been a priest! Never a cat killed a mouse but that you felt guilty about it and tried to take the blame. Of all the knights of Arthur's court who were tomcatting about England twenty years ago, why should it be—?"

"But you can't deny that it might have been—"

"No more than you can prove that it *was*," Sir Lionel said. "I've told you before, Bors: Exercise your distempered conscience somewhere else. It bores me." He turned back to Beaufils. "Did your mother tell you the knight's name?"

Beaufils shook his head.

"Then what was your mother's name?" Sir Bors asked.

"I don't know," Beaufils said. "I always just called her Mother."

"I think you're wasting your time, boy," Sir Lionel said frankly. "Your father could be any of two dozen knights I can think of who were, ah, active in those days."

Beaufils was surprised at this, but not discouraged. "Perhaps you're right. But I ought to ask anyway, I think. Can you show me the way to Camelot?"

"Ay, that we can, son," Sir Bors said.

"We'll even take you most of the way," added Sir Lionel. "We're on our way into Wales ourselves, but we can leave you on the Bristol Road, if that's all right with you."

Since Beaufils had never heard of any of those places, they were all equally acceptable. He agreed readily, and they rode on together.

Beaufils parted from Sir Bors and Sir Lionel two days later, and by the time he left their company, he had learned a great deal more about knights. He knew, for instance, about King Arthur—a king was the leader of the whole tribe of people, like the dominant wolf in a pack—and how King Arthur sent his knights out to protect weak people from other people who might want to hurt them. Beaufils didn't understand why people would want to hurt others, but having met two bandits himself, he knew that there were such people. He learned that some knights abused the power of their weapons and armor to hurt the weak—Sir Bors called these people "recreant knights"—and that one of King Arthur's goals was to stop every recreant knight. Beaufils even learned the names of some of King Arthur's best recreant-knight-stoppers: Sir Gawain, Sir Lancelot, Sir Tor, and others.

There were still some things about knights that Beaufils thought strange, of course. The heavy armor they wore still seemed very impractical to him, for instance. Sir Lionel good-naturedly let Beaufils try on his armor one evening, and Beaufils privately thought that the protective covering of metal was not worth the bother. He felt like a turtle. Moreover, the knightly games that Sir Lionel called tournaments, in which knights bashed their best friends from horses, seemed very odd to Beaufils at first. But then Sir Lionel told how the ladies of the court all attended these games, and Beaufils understood. He had watched young bucks butt heads and cross antlers to impress females before.

At any rate, if Sir Bors and Sir Lionel were what knights were like, Beaufils was pleased that his father was one. He liked the brothers, though they were as different as they could be. He liked their wish to help others and their commitment to their promises (Sir Bors called this "honor"). So it was with a sense of pleasant anticipation that Beaufils rode alone down the road that Sir Lionel had told him would lead to Camelot and the chance to meet other knights, one of whom was his father. Growing up in his lonely forest, he had never been aware that he was missing anything, but now he found the company of other people to be delightful. Of course, not everyone he had met had been equally amiable, but by and large, people were great fun, and Beaufils could hardly wait to meet some more.

II

A True Christian Knight

Beaufils met his next people that very evening. Riding through a wooded area at dusk, he smelled wood smoke through the trees and immediately turned Clover toward the scent. Soon he came to a small fire in a clearing. There was no one by the fire, but Beaufils saw at once that he had come to the camp of two knights. There were two neat bundles of gear, both containing some pieces of armor, and through the trees Beaufils could make out the outlines of two horses, tethered away from the fire. With a smile, Beaufils dismounted from Clover and called out, "Hello, knights."

The bushes to his left moved slightly, and a knight stepped into the clearing. Beaufils was unloading his few things from Clover's back, but he stopped to examine this new person with interest. Beaufils had noticed that people looked different at different ages. The man in the forest, with the white hair and the lined face, Beaufils now realized, had been quite old. Sir Bors and Sir Lionel had been older than Beaufils but younger than the old man in the forest. This knight, however, had smooth cheeks and shining black hair, and looked as if he were about Beaufils's own age.

"What are you doing, boy?" the young knight asked.

"Unloading my things, boy," Beaufils replied, smiling.

"What did you call me?"

"Boy. It's what you called me, isn't it?"

"Yes, but . . ." the young knight trailed off.

"Aren't we nearly the same age?" Beaufils asked.

"I suppose we are, but . . ." Again the young knight hesitated. "Why are you unloading your things?"

"It would be uncomfortable for Clover to bear them all night while I slept."

The young knight looked surprised. "Do you mean to camp here?"

"Yes," Beaufils replied. While he had talked, Beaufils had been looking around for the second knight. Now he located him, just a faint shadow hiding in the bushes at Beaufils's back. Beaufils was just about to say hello when the bushes rustled and the second knight leaped out, swinging his sword toward Beaufils's head. Beaufils was still unloading his gear and happened to have just picked up the cudgel he'd taken earlier from the bandit, so when the new knight swung his sword, Beaufils rapped it sharply to one side with his cudgel and stepped out of its way. The sword missed. The new knight said a word that Beaufils had never heard, then whirled around, raising his sword high above his head and chopping down at Beaufils again. Once again, Beaufils knocked the sword aside, and it dug into the earth by his feet. Beaufils put his foot against the flat of the sword, then stepped down hard, forcing the rest of it to the ground and out of the knight's grasp. The knight snarled at him and stooped down to grab the sword again, but then the first knight stepped between them. "What are you doing, Mordred? This boy has done you no harm!"

The second knight rose slowly to his feet, and the anger disappeared from his face, leaving behind an expression of innocent surprise. "Why, I saw him take up that club, and I thought he was about to strike you, Galahad. Why else should I have attacked him? Aren't you the one who said he might be a bandit?"

"I never said to attack him from behind!"

The two knights stared at each other for a tense moment, and then Beaufils began to laugh. "You thought I was a *bandit?*" The idea seemed very ridiculous.

"Yes, of course," the knight called Mordred said.

"It makes no difference what you thought, Mordred," the knight called Galahad said, still staring hard at the other knight. "To use a sword against a mere boy armed with only a stick is a craven deed. You are lucky you didn't hurt him, for that would have been a mortal sin."

Beaufils didn't know what Galahad had meant by "mortal sin," but he had to chuckle again at the rest of this speech. "Oh, it wasn't *lucky* that he missed me," Beaufils pointed out. "He tried his best."

Mordred's eyes blazed angrily at this, but Beaufils ignored him. Stepping off Mordred's sword, he picked it up and handed it back to the knight. "Here you go, knight. Or should I call you Mordred?"

"'Sir Knight' will do," Mordred said, a bit sharply. "It will help you to remember your place, boy."

Beaufils was about to ask what Mordred meant by this when the other knight spoke. "In truth you are right, boy. He tried to strike you but could not. I have never seen anyone move as quickly as you did. Have you been trained for war?"

Beaufils shook his head. "I don't *think* so," he said. "Have you?" he asked, hoping that Galahad would explain what he meant by "war."

Galahad nodded. "From childhood, I have done nothing else but prepare for one sort of war or another. I have trained my body, my mind, and my soul for battle, both earthly and spiritual."

This didn't help at all, but Beaufils decided he could

ask about this "war" some other time, so he replied politely, "That must have been nice."

Galahad blinked at this, then said, "Come, boy, and join our camp." Mordred started to speak, but Galahad said, "After all, Mordred, having attacked him without cause, we should make amends in whatever way we can. If you don't like it, you can go find another camp. I was here first anyway." He sat down at the fire and gestured for Beaufils to join him. "Mordred and I just met here a few minutes before you came. What is your name?"

"Beaufils. And yours is Galahad? Or should I call you *Sir* Galahad?" Beaufils had learned from Sir Bors and Sir Lionel that people usually used that title of respect with knights.

"No," Galahad said, with an air of regret. "I have not been knighted yet."

Beaufils absorbed this. "So people who are not knights are *made* knights? Who can be made a knight?"

Mordred laughed derisively. "Not a churl like you, if that's what you mean."

"Who then?" Beaufils asked.

"It is customary that only the sons of knights may become knights," Galahad explained gently.

"Oh," Beaufils said. "That's all right then. I don't know that I *want* to be a knight, of course, but it's nice to know that I can become one if I wish."

The two travelers stared at Beaufils in silence for a moment. "Do you mean to say that your father is a knight?" Galahad asked. Beaufils nodded. "What knight?"

"I don't know his name," Beaufils said. Then he told them how his mother had revealed to him before she died that his father was a knight from Camelot who didn't even know that Beaufils had been born.

Mordred laughed again. He was somehow able to make all the sounds of laughter without communicating any feeling of merriment. Beaufils thought it uncanny and not very pleasant. "You don't really expect us to believe that, do you?" Mordred asked. "Your mother was lying to you, boy—trying to make herself more important than she was." Galahad said nothing, but his eyes were wide as he stared at Beaufils. Mordred glanced at Galahad, then said, "Come, Galahad, you aren't going to believe this whelp, are you?"

"Why should the boy's story be a lie?" Galahad said softly. "It is my story as well."

Beaufils had been about to reply sternly to Mordred, whose scorn for his mother had aroused an unfamiliar stirring of anger, but at Galahad's reply Beaufils forgot his irritation.

"Truly? Is your father a knight from Camelot too?"

Galahad nodded. "And my father, like yours, does not know I exist."

Beaufils smiled widely. "Why, we could be brothers!"

"If so," Mordred said, his lips curled in an unpleasant expression, "you can both be very proud of your sire. A busy knight, it seems."

Galahad turned red but didn't reply. Beaufils asked, "And are you on your way to Camelot, like me? To find your father?"

"I am," Galahad said.

Mordred gave his joyless laugh again. "A family reunion, I perceive. I do hope your father is, ah, pleased to see you both."

"Oh, it might not be the same knight, you know," Beaufils assured him. "Sir Lionel said that my father could be one of two dozen knights. He didn't think I would be able to find him at all." He looked at Galahad. "How will you find *yours*?"

"My mother said he would know my name when I was presented to the court. And what about you? Will your father know your name?"

Beaufils shook his head. "I don't know. In fact, I'm not even sure that 'Beaufils' *is* my name. It means 'fair son,' and it was just what Mother called me."

"How pathetic," Mordred said. "Two bast—ah, two *love children*, looking for their fathers."

Galahad's face grew tight. "Why do you sneer at us so, Mordred? Do you think it a weakness in us that we do not know our fathers?"

"No," Mordred replied softly. "I think it a weakness that you seek them out. If I had a father at Camelot who did not know I existed, I would not seek him; I would make him seek me. Then I would make him pay."

Beaufils looked at Mordred in silence, feeling a chill of something black and heavy behind these words. Beaufils had never encountered such a feeling before—a hungry, bitter, and arid emotion that seemed to bleed all the warmth from Mordred's voice when he spoke. Beaufils felt instinctively that he was in the presence of a much greater wickedness than mere bandits with cudgels. Galahad must have sensed it, too, because neither he nor Beaufils spoke to Mordred again that evening as they sat around the fire, then prepared for sleep. When they awoke the next day, Mordred was gone.

Galahad, Beaufils learned as they rode together toward Camelot, had spent all his youth in a place called a convent, where his mother was something called a nun.

"What is that?"

"A nun? Do you not know?" Galahad asked. Beaufils shook his head. "A nun is a bride of Christ, a woman who has wedded herself to Our Lord in mystic union and spends her days meditating on His goodness."

"Oh," Beaufils said. His mother had told him about God and Christ, but he wasn't sure how Christ, whom he knew as a strong presence in moments of great peace, could be married to someone. "And a convent is where Christ's brides live?" he asked.

"Yes. My mother went there after I was conceived, seeking a place away from the world in which to raise me."

Beaufils understood that. It was exactly what his own mother had done, except that his mother had gone farther afield.

Galahad continued. "There I was raised by all the sisters of the convent, taught to give myself to prayer and to the service of God, and then—when I was old enough—trained to use the broadsword."

"Your mother taught you that?" Beaufils asked, mildly interested. When he was with Sir Bors and Sir Lionel, he had lifted Sir Lionel's heavy sword, and he knew that his own mother would not have been strong enough to ply such a weapon. "A strong, burly woman, was she?"

"No, of course not!" Galahad said. "There was a priest nearby who had once been a knight, and he taught me to use sword and shield."

"That was kind of him," Beaufils said, thinking how nice it would have been to have had neighbors himself. "So where *are* your sword and shield?"

Galahad lifted his chin. "I have none. Father Calchis

trained me with his own rusted sword and shield, but they are so old and chipped now that they cannot be used. Mother says that God will provide arms for me."

"That will be nice," Beaufils replied. "Will he give you one of those pointed things—a lance—as well?"

Galahad flushed and turned sharply, but before he could speak Beaufils said, "Why is there a man up in that tree ahead?"

Galahad turned back and stared down the path. A large chestnut tree growing just off the path sent out several long branches, one of which overhung the road a short distance ahead of them. "I see no man," he said.

"He's on the branch over the road, just where the leaves are thickest," Beaufils said. "You don't see his outline through the shadows?"

"I see nothing," Galahad said impatiently.

"I'll show you," Beaufils offered. Sliding from Clover's back, he stepped into the bushes beside the path and made his way to the trunk of the tree. It was an old tree with low branches, ridiculously easy to climb, and it took Beaufils only a few seconds to reach the base of the overhanging branch. There he was, a man in knight's armor, sword in hand, his face turned toward where Galahad sat on his horse. Beaufils waited for the knight to say hello, but the man was so focused on Galahad that he hadn't even heard Beaufils climb the tree beside him. "Hello, knight," Beaufils said at last.

The man jumped in the air, exclaimed something in a sharp voice, and swung his sword blindly behind him in the direction of Beaufils. "Be careful," Beaufils said, evading the sword easily. "You'll fall."

The man fell. His violent swing completely overbalanced him, and he tumbled with a clatter to the path. Beaufils swung down, hung from the branch for a moment, then dropped lightly beside the stunned knight. The knight's sword lay on the ground at Beaufils's feet, and he picked it up. The knight groaned and sat up just as Galahad cantered near.

"What meant thou, Sir Knight," Galahad said, in a somewhat deeper voice than his normal one, "lying thus in wait for strange knights errant?"

The knight shook his head slowly, as though to clear it, then replied, "Are you Sir Breunis Sans Pité?" he asked.

"I am not," replied Galahad.

The knight sighed with relief and rose to his feet. "I beg your pardon," he said. "I had heard that that most wicked of recreant knights was in these parts. He lives but to strike down young knights from ambush, and when I heard you approach, I hid."

"You should not run from recreant knights!" Galahad said sternly.

"But Sir Breunis Sans Pité is a demon with a sword! I confess that I feared for my life."

"You need not fear now that I am with you," Galahad said.

The knight looked Galahad over frankly. "But . . . forgive me for pointing this out . . . you don't seem to be armed."

Galahad lifted his chin. "Sword or no sword, I fear no recreant knight."

"That's admirable," the knight replied. "But if it's all the same to you, I'd rather have my sword back." He glanced at Beaufils, who returned his sword. Immediately the knight grasped the sword by the hilt and put the point at Galahad's throat.

"You are very brave, youngster. Also very stupid. Allow me to introduce myself. I am Sir Breunis Sans Pité, and I am the last knight you will ever see alive."

"You would strike down a knight with no sword?" Galahad asked, his face calm.

"Not extremely clever, are we? Didn't you hear my name? 'Sans Pité' means without mercy. I don't care if you're armed or not, except that unarmed is easier. Are you ready to die now?"

By way of answer, Galahad—who had silently slipped his foot from his stirrup while Sir Breunis talked— simply kicked Sir Breunis in his elbow and, in the same motion, threw himself backward from his horse. He landed on the ground like a cat and whirled around to face the knight, but there was no danger there. Sir

Breunis's sword had flown harmlessly from his grasp, and he was kneeling on the ground clutching his right arm. Galahad retrieved the sword, then strode over to the kneeling knight and placed the edge against his neck. "Tell me why I should not slay you now," Galahad said calmly.

"You've broke my arm!" Sir Breunis said.

"It's true," Beaufils contributed. "I heard it crack. That'll smart for a bit."

"I care not. He would have killed us both. Truly I should break his neck and rid the world of an evil man."

"You would kill an unarmed knight?" Sir Breunis whimpered.

"It is what *you* meant to do, after all," Galahad replied. "It is no crime to punish evil." He drew back the sword to strike.

His eyes glazed with pain, Sir Breunis managed to say, "I don't suppose it would help to say I was sorry, would it?" He clearly didn't think it would, because he then closed his eyes and braced himself for the blow.

But Galahad had stopped and was staring at Sir Breunis uncertainly. In a low voice, as if speaking to himself, he said, "If he has truly repented and I kill him, then I commit a mortal sin."

Sir Breunis opened his eyes, one at a time. Then suddenly, with his good arm, he began frantically touching his forehead and stomach and both shoulders and

31

muttering, "Domine patris ave Maria plene gratia something something summa pater noster" and several other things like that. Beaufils stared at him with consternation. He appeared to have lost his mind.

But Galahad lowered the sword. "Sir Breunis," he said at last. "I do not know if your repentance is true or not, but if it is not, God will requite you for your falseness. I will not slay you."

Sir Breunis stopped muttering and waving his arm about and let out his breath slowly. "You are a true Christian knight, my lord," he said. Then his eyes rolled up in his head, and he fainted, falling face first into the dust.

Beaufils and Galahad rode away an hour later. Beaufils had set the unconscious knight's broken arm and bound it tightly, and Galahad, after much soul-searching, had returned his sword. Pacing back and forth for a long time, Galahad had fretted aloud about whether he should keep the sword for himself or return it. Beaufils was occupied with Sir Breunis's broken arm and didn't pay a great deal of attention, but in the end Galahad slid the sword back in its owner's scabbard. "For if his repentance was true and I left him defenseless, it could be the same as doing him harm myself," he said. "God shall have to provide me another sword, if it be His will."

Beaufils didn't understand Galahad's scruples, but he was content to let him sort out the matter for himself. Leaving Sir Breunis beside the path, he and Galahad remounted and continued together toward Camelot.

"Galahad?" Beaufils said.

"Yes, Beaufils?"

"You're very quick, too."

They slept that night in a dense forest that Galahad said was less than a day's ride from Camelot. Beaufils was pleased that they were near their goal—he had already traveled over far more country than he would have believed existed—but he would not have minded if the journey had been longer. He liked traveling with a friend.

In the middle of the night, Beaufils was awakened by a strange noise. It sounded like nothing he had ever heard, but among the sounds he knew it was most like the cry of a wounded and frightened animal. He sat up at once in the darkness and waited for the noise to recur. When it did, he realized with surprise that it was coming from Galahad, asleep a few yards away. Taking a smoldering stick from the dying fire, Beaufils blew it into flame and held it over his friend to see if he were hurt, but there were no visible wounds. Galahad's eyes were tightly closed, but his forehead shone with sweat, and he writhed and twisted under his blanket.

Beaufils sat cross-legged beside his friend and waited. Galahad appeared to be ill, and if that was so he needed his sleep, but Beaufils wanted him to have help as soon as he awoke. For nearly an hour Galahad moaned and cried out and mumbled to himself, but never did he awake. At last he seemed to grow quieter and to rest more easily and, after waiting another minute, Beaufils turned back toward his own bed, then started with surprise. Seated on a stone beside his bed was an old man.

"You're very quiet, old man," Beaufils said.

"I have that reputation," the man replied. "How is your friend?"

"I hardly know. He seems to be resting better now, but I don't know what was wrong with him. I suppose he is ill, like my mother."

"Your mother is no longer ill," the old man said. "Nor for that matter is Galahad. He was dreaming." Beaufils wanted to ask the man how he knew about his mother, but the man spoke first. "In Galahad's dream, a strange woman came to him. She held out her hands to him in welcome, but he ran away. As he ran, he came to a great tournament of knights. He joined the contest and fought very well, defeating every knight and claiming the crown, but when he knelt to receive his prize, he found it was held by the woman he had run from."

It didn't occur to Beaufils to doubt the old man or even to wonder how he knew Galahad's dream. Instead he said, "Why did Galahad run from the woman?"

The old man nodded. "He was frightened of her."

"She didn't *sound* frightening," Beaufils said.

"To you she would not be," the old man said. "But enough about Galahad. How are you finding your life outside the forest?"

"I like it very much. People are much more interesting than beasts. I never knew how exciting they would be."

"All of them?"

Beaufils shook his head slowly, thinking of Mordred. "Not all, no," he admitted.

"That young knight who was with Galahad?" the old man asked. Beaufils nodded, and the old man seemed satisfied. He rose to his feet. "Son, I must ask you a favor."

"Of course, old man."

"Don't tell anyone you have spoken with me."

"If you wish," Beaufils said. "Why not?"

"Some people might not believe that you met an old man in the forest—or approve of it if they did."

"All right," Beaufils said. "Will we meet again?" The old man nodded, and Beaufils said, "I'm glad to hear it. My name is Beaufils."

"No, it isn't," the old man replied. "But it will do. My name is Scotus." Then he stepped backward and the dark swallowed him completely. Beaufils lay down and went to sleep at once.

Galahad had dark circles under his eyes the next morning, but Beaufils said nothing about his friend's fitful sleep. Since he had promised not to tell Galahad about Scotus, it was best not to say anything at all, even when Galahad stared morosely at the fire and replied irritably to every word. When they had eaten, finishing off the last of the nuts and vegetables that Beaufils had packed for his journey, Galahad spoke suddenly. "We must find a church before we go to Camelot. It has been five days since I've heard mass. I will not go to court until I do." As usual, Beaufils didn't know what Galahad was talking about, but he had no objection to a side trip. So far, everywhere had proven to be equally interesting, and he supposed that a church must be an enjoyable place too.

And so it was. Around midmorning, Galahad spotted a tower that he somehow knew was a church. As they rode near, Galahad tried to explain to Beaufils what he would find there. Beaufils listened closely but it all sounded very strange to him—stranger even than the first description of "knights" that he had heard—and he decided he would just have to wait to see it all himself. Galahad led him up to a huge town filled with more people than Beaufils had ever imagined living in one place—as many as thirty, or even more. Beaufils wanted to stop and talk to them all, especially the children, but Galahad rode through the town without giving the people a glance, went right to the building with the tower, and found a man in black robes. Within an hour Beaufils was sitting in the back of a large room, listening to the pleasing drone of the robed man's murmur while Galahad knelt at the man's feet. There was a sweet, burning smell in the room and dozens of little fires flicking shadows on the walls, and as Beaufils watched the priest and Galahad go through the obviously memorized motions, he felt suddenly peaceful. It made him want to say thank you to God, so he did, but he took care to do so very quietly. Everything seemed to follow such a strict order in the church, Beaufils wasn't sure if giving thanks to God would be allowed.

When the two men were done, Galahad rose to his feet, looking calm and refreshed, and strode back to where Beaufils sat waiting. "I am ready now, my friend," he said. "Let us go to Camelot."

III

A Chair, a Sword, and a Platter

Beaufils was speechless. He had thought that the town where Galahad had gone to church had been large, but Camelot—Camelot was beyond anything he had ever imagined. There were people everywhere, like leaves in a forest, and every one was different and interesting. There were more houses than he had thought could exist, all clustered around high stone walls, and inside the walls, towers rose high in the air, decked with strips of cloth attached to poles and fluttering in the wind. In the streets were wonders beyond compare: there were wooden platforms on wheels being pulled along by mules or horses or some other animals—what a clever idea!—and men with huge muscles and heavy hammers pounding pieces of red-hot metal into shapes—whoever first thought of that?—and other people with

whole tables piled high with vegetables, more than anyone could eat at one time. Beaufils wanted to stop everywhere to talk to the people he met, but Galahad rode
through the town without looking at the people at all, so
Beaufils had to be content with staring at everything as
he passed by.

They came to a great gate, where Galahad spoke to a
man carrying a long pole with a sharp metal point—
a lance, Beaufils supposed—and a moment later they
rode into the castle itself. By this time, Beaufils was too
dazed to take it all in; there were just too many colors,
too much activity, too many faces, for him to register
everything. But then he looked down into the eyes of a
red-haired girl, who was staring at him. "Hello, girl,"
Beaufils said.

The girl turned red and beamed at him. "Good day,
sir," she replied breathlessly.

Another girl, with yellow hair, came up behind the
first girl and stopped. She too was staring at Beaufils, so
he smiled at her, and she turned red, too. "What is your
name?" Beaufils asked the first girl.

"Maggie, sir," the red-haired girl said.

"And I'm Anna," said the yellow-haired girl.

"He didn't ask for *your* name," Maggie said over her
shoulder. "He was talking to me."

"Don't be a piggie," Anna said.

"I saw him first," snapped Maggie.

39

"What does that have to say to anything?" Anna hissed. "You don't think he likes you best just because he saw you first, do you?"

"No, I think so because he spoke to me first," retorted Maggie.

Beaufils didn't understand what was going on, but he realized that somehow he had caused these two girls to speak angrily to each other. Perhaps he had been rude by speaking to only one of them. He said, "I'm very glad to meet you both," smiled at them again, then urged Clover ahead so as to catch up with Galahad. Behind him, he heard Maggie say, "See what you done? You run him off!"

It seemed there were many customs that he would have to figure out in a big town like Camelot, and he hoped he wouldn't make too many more mistakes. He didn't want to make people argue. Galahad stopped and glanced over his shoulder at Beaufils. "Say, Beaufils, do you see the stables anywhere? We ought to put up our horses . . . er, our animals."

Evidently a stable was a place to put horses and mules. Beaufils didn't know where one was or even what one looked like, but he said, "I can ask this girl if you like." He turned to a girl with very dark eyes who had been walking beside him for a little ways, glancing frequently up at him. "Excuse me, girl."

The girl turned red. Evidently turning red was good

manners. Beaufils hoped he didn't have to learn how to do it. She bent her knees and picked up her skirts in an odd gesture, then stammered, "Yes, sir?"

"What is your name?"

"Maude, sir."

"I'm glad to meet you." The girl turned even brighter red, and Beaufils continued. "Can you tell my friend and me where a stable is?"

"Ooh, yes sir," the girl said. "I'd be happy to take you there, sir."

"That's very kind of you," Beaufils replied. "Galahad, Maude here is going to show us the way."

By the time they arrived at the stable, Maude had been joined by three other girls, all eager to help. At the stable, Galahad cared for his great horse while Beaufils and the four girls saw to it that Clover was rubbed down and fed. Girls seemed to like mules more than horses. When they were done, Galahad looked disdainfully at the girls gathered around Beaufils and said, "Perhaps you could ask your, ah, acquaintances if they know when the next meeting of Arthur's Round Table is to be."

Beaufils turned to the girls, who all began talking at once. At last, Maude managed to silence the others and say, "Why, it's tonight, sir. There's a special meeting to discuss the chair! There's going to be a banquet for all the knights of the court in the Great Hall—which Lisa and Martha did ought to be going off to prepare, them

41

bein' kitchen maids—and then the knights'll all go to the Round Table and talk about what's to be done about the chair."

"What chair?" demanded Galahad.

Maude replied at once, but to Beaufils instead of to Galahad. "Ooh, don't you know about the chair? It's the greatest marvel anyone hereabouts has ever seen! It just appeared yesterday, a new chair at the Round Table, with letters carved right in the back of it. They do say that those letters spell out that only the greatest knight ever can sit in that chair, and nobody knows where it came from, with words and everything!"

"Words right on a chair?" Beaufils said. "What a notion!"

"This is a marvel indeed," Galahad said. "And who may go to the banquet?"

"Every knight who's at court'll be there," Maude said.

"We must attend, Beaufils," Galahad said decisively.

"Fine with me," Beaufils replied. "What's a banquet?"

Beaufils followed Galahad around the court for an hour as his friend talked to different knights and other gorgeously dressed people, who Beaufils learned were called "courtiers," and at the end of it all, the two were given a room to share. They entered the room, and Galahad firmly closed the door, shutting out several girls who had been following along to help.

"You should be careful there, my friend," Galahad said soberly.

Beaufils had been about to sit down, but at Galahad's warning he stopped. "Does this chair not look strong enough?" he asked.

"Not the chair, Beaufils. I mean the girls."

Beaufils frowned uncertainly. "Who should be careful? Me or the girls?"

"You, my friend. You are very innocent, I know, and you employ no arts to attract them, but attract them you do. You must keep your distance. Women are more dangerous than you know."

It was inconceivable to Beaufils that the girls who had been so helpful all day long could be dangerous, but he decided not to ask for an explanation. He had learned in his days with Galahad that it was just when his friend was most earnest that he was least likely to make sense.

Galahad continued. "You are wholly unaware of it, Beaufils, but as those girls' attention shows, you are an extraordinarily handsome young man. Your features, your form, and your expression are all perfection itself."

"Please, what does 'handsome' mean?" Beaufils didn't remember his mother ever using that word.

"It means . . . it means pleasant to look at."

As Beaufils had expected, Galahad's explanation made no sense. Beaufils thought that everyone he'd met was pleasant to look at. One person had particularly bright eyes; another had brilliant hair; another smiled with great sweetness; another looked very strong and healthy. Everyone he'd seen had been interesting. But he didn't pursue the subject. Instead he asked, "And are we to go to this big meal—this banquet?"

"Yes," Galahad said. "Do you remember that large knight with the graying beard? That was Sir Kai, the king's seneschal. I told him that I was from a knightly family, which is the truth, and had just arrived in court, and he said that he would see there was a place for me. I"—Galahad faltered—"I don't know if there will be a seat for you. I think that Sir Kai assumed you were my squire. Your deerskin clothes, you know, don't look much like knight's garments. But we'll go together and see if there's a place for you."

When they arrived at the Great Hall that evening, Beaufils was so overwhelmed by the throng of gaily clad knights and ladies and the confusion of helpers bearing trays of food that he couldn't imagine how anyone could find a seat at all. But the other people seemed to have an instinct that told them how to find a place—like the instincts that teach birds how to make nests and fly south at wintertime. Even Galahad seemed to have this innate ability, for he found a chair almost at once, near the end of one of the long tables. Beaufils, however, was soon lost in the crowd. Every time he saw an empty chair, someone else sat in it before he got to it. At last he saw one more empty chair, one that no one else was moving toward. It looked very uncomfortable, which probably explained why it had been left for last, but Beaufils decided not to worry about all the shiny yellow and red and green knobs that stuck out of the back. He didn't have to lean back against them, after all. With a quick skip and a hop he came to the chair and climbed over the great yellow armrests into the seat.

The room grew suddenly quiet. Looking up, Beaufils saw that every face was turned toward him. He smiled. "Hello, knights and ladies," he said.

The large knight whom Galahad had mentioned earlier, Sir Kai, rose to his feet, his face stern, and opened his mouth to speak, but just then a door creaked open behind Beaufils and the knight was still. Beaufils sensed someone walking up beside his chair, and he looked over his shoulder to see a slender man with a gray beard regarding him curiously.

"Hello, old man," Beaufils said.

"Hello, er, young man," the man replied. His face was lined, as if he was often sad, but when he spoke his eyes glinted with humor and little lines appeared at the corners of his eyes.

"My liege—" began Sir Kai.

"Peace, Kai," the man said, holding up one hand. He looked back at Beaufils. "Are you, er, comfortable, lad?"

"Not very. This is a terrible chair. Look at all these bumps in the back."

"I quite agree," the man said gravely, stilling the murmur that had risen at Beaufils's words. "A most inconvenient place to put rubies and emeralds."

"I suppose that's why this was the last chair left open," Beaufils said.

The man pursed his lips. "Well, perhaps there's another reason, too. You see, the way these dinners work at Camelot is that this chair is reserved for the person who directs the meal."

"Oh," Beaufils said. "What does that mean?"

"Well, the one who sits there tells everyone when they may begin eating, for example."

Beaufils blinked. "I didn't realize that when I sat here."

The man smiled. "No, I didn't think you did."

Beaufils returned his smile, then looked around the room at the crowd. "But I don't mind doing it. Let's start eating, shall we?"

The room was silent. Two or three of the knights were smiling, but the rest only stared at Beaufils. No one began eating. Beaufils looked up at the old man. "Did I do it wrong?"

The man suddenly gave Beaufils a wide, boyish grin, and Beaufils realized that he was not as old as he had thought. "Why, no, you did beautifully, lad." The man looked at the others. "Well, you heard him, didn't you?"

Dazedly, and in silence, the knights and ladies began

to fill their plates from the platters that lay on the table. Beaufils looked gratefully up to the gray-bearded man. "Thank you," he said. "I wouldn't have known what to do without your help."

"Do you know," the man said thoughtfully, "there may be some other customs that come up that you will need help with. Perhaps it would be a good idea if I sat beside you."

"I'd like that very much," Beaufils said. "But there's no chair."

"Perhaps one could be fetched."

"Yes, that would be good," Beaufils agreed. "Why don't you go fetch a chair while I make room for you?" He turned to the lady who was sitting on his left and who was staring at them both. Beaufils met her gaze and said, "I say, lady, would you mind moving over a bit to make room for my friend here?"

The lady looked from Beaufils to the gray-bearded man, then back. The man bowed apologetically to her and said, "If it's not too much trouble, Guinevere."

"It would serve you right if I said no," the lady said to the man, but then, with a sudden chuckle, she began making room for the man at the table. The tension in the room eased, and people began to converse with each other.

When the man had taken his seat beside Beaufils, he said, "I don't believe we've met before, have we?"

"No, I just arrived at Camelot early this afternoon. What a place it is, too!"

"Does it not meet with your approval?" the man asked.

"Oh, I didn't mean that! It's just that it's so very big, with so many people. I've never been anywhere like it! How can you ever get to know so many?"

"I rather think that most people don't try," the man replied.

Beaufils pondered this. "Doesn't anyone know all the people of Camelot?"

"I doubt it," the man replied. "You see, there are always new ones coming."

"Yes. That's delightful, I imagine, but it *will* make it harder," Beaufils said reflectively. "You see, I'm trying to find one particular person, and if no one knows everyone, how will I do it?"

"May I ask whom you are looking for?"

"My father," Beaufils said.

"Your father," the man repeated, his voice dropping so that people nearby could not hear him.

Beaufils nodded. "Yes. Before she died, my mother told me that my father was a knight at Camelot, and she sent me to find him."

"Which knight?" the man asked, so quietly that Beaufils could hardly hear him.

"I don't know," he admitted. "Mother didn't say that, and I didn't know how important the name would be. Now, of course, I see why Sir Lionel said it would be useful to know his name."

"Sir Lionel?"

"Yes, I met him and Sir Bors on my way here. They gave me directions."

The man nodded. "I believe I shall accept that as a recommendation. We shall take up your matter after dinner, at the meeting of the Round Table."

"Do you think you may be able to help me, then?"

"I shall do my best."

"Perhaps you could ask King Arthur if he knows?" Beaufils suggested.

The man hesitated, then said, "Actually, lad, I *am* King Arthur."

Beaufils looked at him blankly for a moment, then began to laugh. "Of course. Now I understand. I'm sitting in your chair, aren't I?"

"Well, yes. You are, a bit."

"That's why it was left by the others."

King Arthur nodded, grinning impishly.

"Would you like to trade back?"

"Not at all. This chair is much more comfortable, and I don't have those dreadful high armrests between me and my wife. May I offer you some bread . . . er, what is your name?"

"My mother called me Beaufils. And yes, I'd love some."

King Arthur turned to the lady at his side and said, "Guinevere, allow me to introduce you to Beaufils."

"It means 'fair son,'" Beaufils explained, smiling a greeting at the lady.

"Well, your mother was right about that, anyway," Guinevere replied frankly. "The 'fair' part, I mean. Do you have any idea how handsome you are, Beaufils?"

"I don't *think* so," Beaufils replied. "Is it something that I need to learn right away? You see, I have so much to learn about living among people that I have to put less important things aside for now."

"I think you can wait on that one," King Arthur said. "Some butter?"

The dinner took an amazingly long time. Beaufils had had his fill and stopped eating long before the others were done. At last, at King Arthur's prompting, Beaufils signaled an end to the dinner, and all the knights rose and followed the king through a doorway into another large room. This room was a perfect circle, and at the very center was a huge round table with chairs spaced about it. The knights went immediately to particular seats, but Beaufils held back. He wasn't going to be caught sitting in someone else's chair again. When all the knights were seated and only a few chairs were left empty, he went to join a cluster of courtiers and other people who stood along one side of the room. Beaufils saw Galahad among them.

From his place at the table, King Arthur addressed the assembled knights and courtiers. "Thank you, all, for coming at such short notice. It seemed to me and to my counselors that the matter of this chair should be dealt with at once rather than be left for our next gathering." There were many nodding heads, and whispering voices buzzed in the room. King Arthur waited until these had subsided, then continued. "Before we deal with the chair, though, one smaller matter has come to my attention. Beaufils, would you stand beside me, please?"

Beaufils stepped out of the knot of standing observers and joined the king.

"This young man, who so ably presided over our dinner, is named Beaufils. He comes here, vouched for by Sir Lionel and Sir Bors of our fellowship, with a question to ask. Beaufils, would you tell my knights why you are here?"

Beaufils smiled at the king. "Thank you, King Arthur." He looked back up at the knights. "I'm here to find my father," he said.

The knights were very quiet.

Beaufils went on. "You see, until just a few days ago, I lived with my mother, but she became ill. When she saw that she would die soon, she called me to her and told me that my father was a knight at Camelot. She said she lived here in the days before I was born, but when she discovered that she had conceived, she left. She went to a forest and gave birth to me, and we'd lived there ever since. But she told me I should not live entirely alone, so she sent me to find my father."

All the knights at the table looked around at each other. At last the large knight whom King Arthur had called Kai spoke to the king. "My liege, may I ask this youngster some questions?"

"Respectfully, yes."

Kai looked at Beaufils. "Since you didn't say it earlier, I gather that you don't know your father's name?"

"No, I don't. Mother didn't say."

"What was your mother's name?"

Beaufils shook his head. "I don't know that either. I always just called her Mother."

"You never heard anyone else call her by name?"

"I never *saw* anyone else until a few days ago."

"Good Gog," Kai said, a reluctant smile growing on his face. "Never?" Beaufils shook his head. "What forest is this?"

"What do you mean?" Beaufils asked.

"What is it called?"

Beaufils stared at him. "Do *forests* have names, too?" It seemed very funny to him, but he held back his laughter. "I didn't know that."

Kai gaped at him for a moment, then asked, "How old are you?"

"Seventeen, maybe?"

"Maybe?"

"I don't know that either," Beaufils admitted. "It never seemed very important in the forest, you see."

Kai blinked, then said, "Beaufils, hey? That's French for 'fair son,' isn't it? She should have called you 'fair mystery' instead. What would that be in French?"

One of the men standing at the edge of the room, near Galahad, stepped forward, clearing his throat loudly. "That, Sir Kai, would depend on whether you chose to use the archaic French that is still found in court documents or the more colloquial dialect in common use, the *romanische,* as it is called."

Kai rolled his eyes and said, "Lord, who invited the scholar to this meeting?"

King Arthur replied gently, "I asked Clerk Geoffrey if he would join us tonight, Kai."

The scholar continued. "If you use the archaic speech, then 'fair mystery' might be Le Beau Desconus, but in the dialect one might rather say Le Bel Inconnu."

"Would it make any difference if I said I didn't really want to know and was sorry I asked?" Kai said.

"In this case, given the boy's mixed parentage, with a noble father and a commoner mother, either rendering might be defensible," the scholar concluded.

At that point a knight with a bushy red beard spoke. "Just a moment, Geoffrey. I'm not certain that the boy's mother was a commoner." He turned to Beaufils. "Your speech is cultured, Beaufils, like that of an educated man, and your mother called you by a French name."

"Please, knight," Beaufils asked. "What do you mean 'educated'?"

The knight grinned. "Yes, I can see that might be a new concept to one raised alone in the woods. One advantage of your childhood would be that you escaped education."

"But what *is* education?"

"It's a horrible time when you sit in a bleak room wishing to be outside while dusty old people try to teach you to read and do sums and so on."

"Oh, I can read," Beaufils said. "Mother taught me how." Then he frowned and added, "But she must have done it wrong, because I thought it was fun."

The red-bearded knight nodded solemnly. "Yes, I'm afraid she did it wrong. Lucky you." Then he turned to the other knights. "Clearly Le Beau Desconus was born to a lady of good birth who spoke French. Does that help?"

Once again the knights all looked around the table at one another and no one spoke. After a moment the red-bearded knight looked back at Beaufils. "I'm afraid that your father could be any one of several older knights. Thinking back eighteen years, I imagine that I could be your father myself, but I confess I'm reluctant to claim that role without further proof."

At that, King Arthur said, "Perhaps someone would be less reluctant in a private setting. I invite Beaufils to remain at court as long as he wishes, and if you think you might be the man he seeks, you may find him and speak to him alone." The knights seemed to agree with this, and King Arthur looked at Beaufils. "Don't despair, lad. I have a feeling you'll find what you want."

Then the king turned again to the knights. "And now, let us consider the marvelous chair." He waved his hand at an empty chair beside him. "As you know, this marvel appeared in this room by means unknown within the last two days. No one has ever seen it before; no one saw anyone bringing it. The chair is curiously inscribed with a message." The king read from the back of the chair: "'This is the Siege Perilous. Here ought to sit only he who is the purest knight of all.'" The king looked up. "And so I called this meeting to ask your counsel. But," he added, "after I summoned you to the table, we have had a like marvel appear." This took the assembly by surprise, and there was a brief buzz of whispers. The king nodded to Kai, who rose and walked to the wall behind him, pulling a black cloth off a bundle and revealing a sword stuck point down in a slab of stone.

The king said, "This one also bears an inscription: 'Never shall man take me hence, but only he by whose side I ought to hang, and he shall be the best knight in the world.' "

The king was silent for a moment while the knights looked at the sword, then at each other. King Arthur said, "So I ask you. What do we do?"

The red-bearded knight said, "I'm not sure I know what you mean. We have only two options: either we test them or we leave them alone."

"Yes, Gawain," the king said. "But we must think about both options. These marvels are clearly enchantments, and as enchantments they may be either a call to some noble adventure or a trap, devised of evil sorcery."

"There is another possibility, sire," said another of the standing men. This one wore robes of red and gold and had on a funny hat.

"Yes, Bishop Baldwin?"

"This could be a miracle of God, given as a test to your court."

"What sort of test?" the king asked.

"A test of faith, trying whether your knights will risk themselves in the perilous seat and thus earn the blessed sword."

Clerk Geoffrey cleared his throat again and said, "Excuse me, Your Holiness, but I believe you'll find that the word is not 'seat,' but 'siege.' "

Bishop Baldwin looked irritated and said, "And what does 'siege' mean, clerk?"

"It's from the French," the clerk replied. "Both archaic and common, actually."

"I didn't ask where it's from; I asked what it means."

"It . . . it means 'seat.' "

Bishop Baldwin rolled his eyes and turned back toward the king, but the clerk kept talking. "But I should point out that the word 'perilous' is not spelled correctly in French, where it should be written with a different final letter."

"Nobody cares, scholar," Bishop Baldwin said. "O king, I suggest that we give these wonders a trial, to see who has the faith to face a miracle of God."

"And what if the chair and the sword are anointed with a poison that will kill those who touch them?" the king asked mildly. "I do have enemies who are capable of concocting such an ointment, you know. They would love to deprive me of some of my greatest knights."

"Again I say, it is a test of faith," announced Baldwin.

"I say throw them both in the cellars and forget about them," said Kai. Then all the knights began talking at once, each explaining his own view to anyone who would listen. In the hubbub, Galahad stepped out of the cluster of standing courtiers, walked quietly over to the sword, took it by the hilt, and drew it smoothly from the stone. The noise began to subside. Then Galahad stepped up to the chair and sat in it. For a moment the chair glowed with an orange light, then all was still.

King Arthur examined Galahad. "That appears to solve that problem," he said softly, stern eyes resting on Galahad. "What is your name, son?"

Before Galahad could answer, the clerk, who had walked over to examine the chair and the stone, gave a sharp exclamation. "Look, sire! The message on the chair! It's changed!"

"Changed?"

"It's a different inscription, sire! It says, 'This is the siege of Galahad, the Haut Prince.'"

King Arthur looked at Galahad. "Is that your name?"

"It is, sire."

Then another voice spoke. "Did you say 'Galahad'?" Beaufils looked around to see a tall man with glossy black hair and very broad shoulders rising to his feet.

"That is my name," Galahad asserted again.

"What is it, Lancelot?" King Arthur asked, turning to the knight who had just stood.

"Galahad is also one of my names," the knight replied. "A family name. Who is your father, Galahad?"

"I do not know for sure. Like my friend Beaufils, I have come to this court to find him. He is a great knight who sixteen years ago was enchanted into believing that my mother was the woman he loved most in the world. When he woke and found that she was another, he rushed from the room and never discovered that he had begotten a son."

58

The knight called Lancelot looked very sober. "What was your mother's name?"

Galahad looked Lancelot in the eye and said, "Do you not know?"

"Elaine?" Lancelot whispered. Galahad nodded slowly. Lancelot looked at him for a long moment, then said, "And are you indeed my son?"

"If you are that knight, I am."

King Arthur looked from Galahad to Lancelot, then smiled. "If this is so, then it is a cause for rejoicing. We came to discuss two marvels, and we discover a third."

Immediately the room burst into sound, as all the knights exclaimed over the wonders they had seen. Beaufils smiled. It hadn't been hard for Galahad to find his father at all. When the hubbub died down, the king reached from his chair to Galahad's and formally welcomed him to his court. "I shall watch your future with interest," he said. "After all, few knights have come to my court so highly recommended as you."

Bishop Baldwin said loudly, "This is indeed a mark of God's favor, that so young a knight should achieve his miraculous tests and sit in the Siege Perilous! Surely the Spirit's blessing is strong upon this great king and his court!"

Just then, as if prompted by Bishop Baldwin's words, a strange light began filling the room. Beaufils looked around but could not see where the light was coming from. Indeed, it seemed to come from everywhere equally, because there were no shadows. It was as if light had reversed itself: instead of shining outward from one source, it was shining inward from everywhere at once. No one spoke.

Then, as Beaufils breathed deeply of the strange light and the eerie silence, a new sight appeared: a golden platter, like one of the great dishes that had held food for the banquet, but empty. No one carried the platter; it appeared over the center of the table, floating like an airborn dandelion seed. Then, slowly, it began to move around the table, stopping in front of each knight for a moment before moving on, and everywhere it stopped, a plate of food appeared on the table before that knight. When it had gone all around the room, it returned to the center of the table, floated for a moment, then rose to the ceiling and disappeared, like a wisp of smoke.

"A sign from God," whispered Bishop Baldwin.

No one answered for a moment. Then the red-bearded knight, whom King Arthur had called Gawain, said quietly, "Out of curiosity, has everyone else been served the one food that he loves most in the world?" All the knights nodded.

Then the room shook, and a great voice from everywhere said, "This is the Grail. He who finds it will find all he truly desires. It is a quest."

IV

QUESTING

For a very long time after the voice faded and the platter that the voice had called the "Grail" disappeared, no one spoke or moved. At last Beaufils, who had watched the apparition with wonder, said, "Well, that was certainly exciting. Does this sort of thing happen often here at Camelot?"

No one answered, but his calm voice seemed to break the spell that had fallen over the room. The knights began blinking, rubbing their eyes, and shaking their heads, while beside Beaufils, Bishop Baldwin sank slowly to his knees, touching his forehead and shoulders and belly and muttering to himself, just as Sir Breunis Sans Pité had done in the woods. This evidently was a way to pray, but Bishop Baldwin didn't look very peaceful—in fact, he looked terrified. Galahad, on the other hand, was radiant. His eyes gazed at the ceiling where the Grail had disappeared, and his face glowed with wonder and excitement.

King Arthur broke the restless silence. "Well, my friends, today has certainly been a day of wonders, each more astonishing than the last. I'm glad that we're already assembled, because I need your counsel." He paused, smiled lopsidedly and said, "To put it simply, my friends, what did all that mean?"

"The voice called that dish a Grail," one knight said. "What's a Grail?"

A knight with a neat brown beard and a serious face leaned forward. "My liege?" he said.

"Yes, Parsifal?"

"I have some experience with this matter myself, and that did not look like what I know as the Grail."

King Arthur looked surprised. "What experience is this, Parsifal?"

Parsifal looked across the table at the red-bearded knight named Gawain, hesitated, then said, "It was a quest that I followed many years ago—a test that I failed once and then, by grace, was allowed to try again."

"And you've never spoken of this quest at court?" asked the king.

"No, sire. The test I speak of took place in an enchanted castle, in a . . . in a different world from this one."

Beside Beaufils, Bishop Baldwin rose slowly to his feet, and Beaufils heard him whisper, "Sorcery!"

King Arthur asked, "And you encountered the Grail in this enchanted castle?"

"Yes, sire. The Grail is a magical stone that provides food for every banquet in that castle."

"A stone, you say? Not a serving dish?"

"That's right, sire."

The knights spoke in hushed tones to one another while the king frowned thoughtfully. Parsifal waited in silence.

"Then do you say that this vision that we all saw is *not* the Grail?" the king asked.

Before Parsifal could reply, Bishop Baldwin stepped forward. "This is nonsense, sire. We have all seen that the Grail is a serving dish, and the voice of God Himself has told us so. Even if Sir Parsifal believes he is speaking the truth, of which I am not at all certain, he is mistaken. Whatever foul, magical object he may have seen can have nothing to do with this holy Grail."

This seemed so silly that Beaufils had to laugh. All eyes turned toward him, and King Arthur said, "Beaufils?"

"I'm sorry to disturb your council," Beaufils said, still smiling. "But it *did* seem so funny."

"What did you find funny?" asked the king.

"The idea that this Grail had to be one thing or the other," Beaufils explained. "Well, doesn't it seem silly to you? Parsifal says that the Grail he knows provides food, and the Grail that we saw did the same thing. How many other things do you know that do that? The two Grails seem more alike than different, don't they? The only way they're different is how they look, and that can't be very important."

King Arthur smiled, and Kai gave a rumbling laugh. "He's not just a pretty face, I see."

Bishop Baldwin looked at Beaufils very sternly and seemed about to argue further, but then the scholar, Geoffrey, cleared his throat again.

"Yes, Clerk Geoffrey?" King Arthur said.

"Your Highness," Geoffrey said, bowing, "perhaps I may be able to help somewhat. The word 'Grail' is not entirely unknown among scholars."

"What do you know of the Grail?" the king asked.

"It is an ancient word, although its origin is still disputed by many. Some scholars, noting that in some documents it is spelled with a double 'a'—that is, g-r-a-a-l—suggest that its origin should be sought in some heathenish Germanic tongue, such as that spoken by the Alemanni or the Visigoths, of which the Roman historian Tacitus has given us so thorough a description. If so, it is proposed that the word should have the meaning 'bowl.' This, however, has been disputed by many other scholars who are themselves regrettably

German, and whose objectivity must thereby be held to be in some question."

Beaufils stared at Geoffrey, fascinated with the droning sound of his meaningless words. It was like listening to a very repetitive night bird sing as you went to sleep. Kai lowered his chin into his hands and stared glumly at the table in front of him.

"It should, however, be noted," Geoffrey said, "that a minority viewpoint considers the word to have sprung from a corrupted spelling of the French word *grêle*, which I hardly need say refers to a hailstorm or even a hail*stone*. I find Sir Parsifal's suggestion that the Grail is a stone to be a significant correlation to this reading."

Beaufils met Gawain's eyes, and the knight grinned at him. "This is what *I* meant by education," the knight said.

"Have you ever heard anyone say so little for so long?" muttered Kai.

Geoffrey ignored them both. "And finally," he said with a flourish, "there is the late view, held by most reputable scholars to be spurious, that the Grail is a vessel of religious significance. Indeed, the monastery just over the hill from Camelot, at Glastonbury, claims to have been founded by none other than Joseph of Arimathea, he who gave a tomb for Our Lord in Jerusalem, and at Glastonbury they say that when Joseph came to our land he brought with him a vessel containing some of the holy blood of Christ. This vessel the monks of Glastonbury call the Holy Grail, or in the old French, the *San Greal*. Rearranging the letters of these words, though, one finds a secondary meaning: *sang real*, which is French for 'True Blood.' "

Beaufils smiled broadly, "Oh, I get it," he said. "It's like a word game! How clever!"

No one paid any attention to Beaufils, because Bishop Baldwin had grown very excited and was shouting, "At last we know! It is the Cup of Our Lord's Last Supper! Containing the Holy Blood!"

Geoffrey looked pained and cleared his throat again. Beaufils wondered if his throat got sore from all that gurgling. "As I *thought* I had made plain, most scholars today find the religious interpretation of the word to be pure fiction. To put it bluntly, we think the Glastonbury monks made it up."

"Nonsense! You saw it right here, didn't you?" Bishop Baldwin declared, dismissing the clerk with a peremptory wave of his hand. "My liege, God has sent this quest to you. You must send all your knights out at once, to find this Holy Grail!"

A babble of voices followed this pronouncement, but one by one the knights grew silent and turned their eyes toward King Arthur, who did not appear to Beaufils to be very pleased. At last the king said, "What do you say, my knights?"

Gawain rose to his feet. "Arthur, I don't know what this vision means, whether this Grail is holy or unholy or neither one, but this I know: we have received a call to adventure, and I have never refused that call before. I will seek this Grail."

One by one other knights rose to their feet, until well over half of them stood with Gawain. As each new knight stood, King Arthur's face seemed to grow sadder. "I seem to be losing most of my knights," he said at last.

"I'm staying here," announced Kai.

"I, too," added Parsifal. "I've already found my Grail, after all."

The other knights who had remained seated nodded. One of them was Galahad's father, Lancelot, who said, "I will stay with you as well, O king."

"No!" exclaimed Galahad, shocked and disappointed. "Not you! Is my own father afraid of this quest?"

Lancelot turned his head and looked at his son calmly. "If you wish to think it, my Galahad. But think what you will, I shall remain with my king. As for you, do what you think best."

Once again, Galahad raised his eyes worshipfully toward the ceiling where the Grail had been. "I will seek the Grail," he said in a ringing voice. "With this sword I have drawn from the stone, I will seek it until either I have found it or have died in the attempt."

In the silence that followed this grand declaration,

Beaufils said, "That sounds nice, Galahad. I'll go with you."

All the knights who had volunteered for the quest— "quest" means "search," Beaufils discovered after asking about—were to set off together the next morning. Alone in their room that night, Galahad and Beaufils agreed that Beaufils would act as Galahad's squire on their journey, which Galahad explained would involve helping out around their camp and taking care of Galahad's armor and sword and shield. Beaufils didn't mind doing that, but he pointed out to Galahad, "You don't have a shield, remember?"

"God shall send one," Galahad said calmly. "Just as He sent a sword."

There was no arguing with that, so Beaufils applied himself to learning how to care for armor.

They set off the next morning with a grand fanfare, and all the questing knights stayed together at first. After an hour or so, Gawain rode a huge black horse up beside Beaufils, who was still on his old friend Clover the mule. "Good morning, lad," Gawain said, smiling. "I gather that you're now young Galahad's squire?"

"That's right," Beaufils said. "Galahad says that all knights have squires, and I don't mind doing my bit for a friend." He glanced around. "Do you have a squire, Gawain?"

Gawain nodded. "Ay, and I'm wishing he were here. His name's Terence, and I'd like him to meet you."

"He's away now?"

"Yes. He, um, has a home in another land, and he's gone to visit his father there."

"Oh? Is his father a knight, too?"

Gawain shook his head. "Nay, his father is . . . well, it's a bit difficult to explain. Terence's father is a great man in that other place, and Terence has gone to ask his father if he has heard any important news."

Gawain seemed to expect a reply, so Beaufils said, "That sounds nice."

Gawain grinned. "You're not even curious about what sort of news he wants?"

"Not really," Beaufils said. "You see, nearly everything's news to me."

Gawain chuckled. "Yes, I imagine so. But I'd like to tell you all the same. Do you mind?"

"Not at all."

Gawain said, "You see, King Arthur is the greatest king this land has ever seen—or ever will see, I imagine— but not everyone wants a great king. A great king protects the humble and suppresses the proud, and that irritates the proud. So the king has powerful enemies who wish him gone, and every year there are revolts against him. Just this past month, word has come of such a plot. Terence's father is a knowledgeable sort of person, so Terence has gone to ask him." Gawain watched Beaufils's face in silence for a moment, then said, "You may be wondering why I'm telling you this."

This question hadn't occurred to Beaufils, but it seemed that Gawain wanted to tell him, so Beaufils asked, "Why?"

"Because, my boy, there is something in your face and the way you move that reminds me of Terence, as if you've come from the same place he does. I was wondering if you'd had any contacts from the people of that world. Tell me, Le Beau Desconus, have you ever met someone who seemed to you to be strange?"

"Everyone's strange to me," Beaufils pointed out.

"I mean someone who looked different from other people and who seemed to know things that other people didn't know and who only appeared to you when you were alone?"

Beaufils hesitated, frowning. Scotus, the old man who had told him about Galahad's dream, had said not to tell others about him.

Gawain was watching Beaufils's face closely, and now he smiled. "Never mind. I think I have my answer. How long have you known Galahad?"

"Just a few days," Beaufils replied. "We met on the way to court."

"He seems a fine lad, though a bit young to be 'the best

knight in the world.' He can't be much more than sixteen. Even Lancelot wasn't called that until he was—"

At that moment Galahad himself rode up and joined them. "Beaufils," Galahad said, interrupting Gawain, "I've been asking the other knights and have learned that there is a church off to the east of us."

"Is there?" Beaufils replied agreeably. "Fancy that."

"I was shocked to see how few of Arthur's great knights joined me for early services this morning before we set out," Galahad said, his lips set disapprovingly. Gawain looked amused but said nothing. Galahad continued. "It is clear that this quest for the Holy Grail can only be achieved by a knight of utter purity, and so it behooves us to make confession as often as we can. Let us turn off this path and go to the church."

Gawain's smile grew. "You confessed before we left this morning and now you want to go confess again? Just what have you been up to over there?"

Galahad scowled but did not look at Gawain. "Come, Beaufils."

"Very well," Beaufils said. "Goodbye, Gawain. I hope we have a chance to talk again."

"I hope so too, lad."

Then Beaufils followed Galahad down a narrow track that led away from the other questing knights and into a thick wood. After nearly two hours, they came to a wooden building. It was small and roughly made, but on its roof was the pointy tower that seemed to be the mark of a church. Murmuring a prayer of thanks, Galahad dismounted and headed for the building. As he approached it, the door opened and two men appeared. One was a knight and the other a priest. Both men stopped, and Galahad bowed deeply to the priest. "Greetings, Father," he said. "I am a knight errant seeking absolution and spiritual guidance from your hand."

The priest looked momentarily flustered but after a moment said, "You are welcome, my son. I shall see to you as soon I bless Sir Brandegoris on his quest."

The knight, Sir Brandegoris, said abruptly, "Who are you? We haven't met, have we?"

"I am Galahad, son of Sir Lancelot," Galahad replied.

"Son of Lancelot? First I've heard of it!"

Beaufils chuckled and commented, "It was the first Lancelot had heard of it, too."

Galahad frowned, making Beaufils wonder if he had said something wrong, but Galahad didn't explain. He said, "I left my noble father at Camelot this morning that I might join the rest of Arthur's knights on the great quest."

"*Great* quest?" exclaimed Sir Brandegoris. "Dash it all, you leave court for a few days and everybody goes off on a quest. Say, they aren't after the Holy Shield of Evelake, are they?"

"Holy shield?" Galahad repeated, his eyes bright.

"Because if they are, they can all just go home again. I'm going to get that one myself."

The priest looked irritated and tried to usher Galahad into the church, but Galahad wouldn't be moved. "What shield is this?" he demanded.

"This priest here was just telling me about it," Sir Brandegoris said. "In the forest just down this path there's a shield hung on a tree. Only the greatest of knights can take that shield down."

"It is a sign from God!" breathed Galahad.

"Maybe so, but not for you," Sir Brandegoris said sharply. "I was here first, and I paid good money for the information."

The priest looked pained. "Please, Sir Brandegoris. You paid for no information. If you chose to make a donation to this church, that is your own affair, but I am no merchant."

"What? Oh, right. Blessed if I didn't forget that. It was a contribution, not a payment, and a jolly steep contribution at that. Oh well, I don't mind. I've plenty of coin." Sir Brandegoris tossed a clinking leather bag up in the air and caught it. The priest's eyes followed it up and down. "Anyway," the knight said, "I'm off to get that shield myself. Shall I bring it back and show you?"

"You must not, Sir Brandegoris!" the priest said hastily. "When this Holy Shield was left there by

King Evelake, son of Joseph of Arimathea himself, he decreed that whoso took it must never use it just to show others its—"

"Joseph of Arimathea!" Galahad said breathlessly. "Truly, it is a sign! I must confess at once!"

"Well, why don't you do that, while I go fetch my new shield?" Sir Brandegoris said. With that, he dropped his bag of coins in his saddlebag, mounted, and rode away, while Galahad followed the priest inside. Beaufils went in for a moment, but this church didn't feel peaceful, like the other one, and after waiting a bit, he strolled back outside to curry Clover and Galahad's horse. He finished, and still Galahad remained inside, so Beaufils stretched out in a sunny spot to think about money.

He had been puzzling about this money for several days, actually. Sir Bors and Sir Lionel had explained to him as they rode together that what the bandits who attacked him had been looking for had been round flat metal things called money, or coins, and that everyone wanted these things. They had tried to explain why, but it had all seemed absurd to Beaufils. Since leaving Sir Bors and Sir Lionel, though, Beaufils had observed the truth of their words. In the marketplace at Camelot, he had seen how highly these round things were esteemed and had even watched a man trade a whole basket of food for just two or three of them. Beaufils had also noticed that some people seemed to feel good about themselves

if they had some of these bits of metal—like Sir Brandegoris tossing his bag of coins up and down with so much
satisfaction—and others, who didn't have as many coins,
seemed to feel unhappy about it—like the priest who
had gazed so hungrily at Sir Brandegoris's bag.

It was all very puzzling, and Beaufils was no closer to
understanding it when at last Galahad and the priest
appeared at the church door. Galahad seemed refreshed,
but the priest looked almost haggard. "Thank you,
Father," Galahad was saying. "I hope I didn't forget to
confess something."

"I can't see how," the priest muttered irritably.
"Unless you left out the sin of making too much of your
own sins."

A cloud flitted across Galahad's brow. "Do you really
think that might be a sin, Father? Do you think I
should—?"

"No, no," the priest said hastily. "Not at all. And if it *is*
a sin, I absolve you of it. No extra charge! Just go, please!"

"If you think that I am truly cleansed," Galahad said.

"Pure as snow!" the priest assured him.

A motion from the right caught Beaufils's eye, and
the horse belonging to Sir Brandegoris appeared, walking back down the trail the knight had taken an hour
before, with Sir Brandegoris himself slumped over the
horse's neck. Galahad cried out and rushed over to the
knight, but the priest only closed his eyes and sighed

75

with frustration. It struck Beaufils that the priest wasn't surprised at all, and that his frustration wasn't because Sir Brandegoris was hurt but because Galahad had seen it.

"Beaufils! Come help me!" Galahad called.

Together, Galahad and Beaufils lowered the knight from his saddle. They removed his helm, and while Galahad examined him, Beaufils studied a deep dent in the back of the helm. Sir Brandegoris moaned and reached up one gauntleted hand to his head. "What happened?" he croaked.

"He clearly was unworthy to take down the Holy Shield of King Evelake," pronounced the priest. "Let it be a warning to all who so presume."

"I never even saw who hit me," Sir Brandegoris said with another groan.

Beaufils took the horse's head and spoke softly to the animal, calming it, and while he stroked its neck, he reached back and felt in the knight's saddlebags. The bag of money was gone.

"You stay here with this good priest," Galahad said, standing suddenly. "I shall seek this shield myself, and if the same enemy attacks me, I shall avenge your humiliation! Come, Beaufils."

Galahad raced to his mount and started at a gallop down the path toward the Holy Shield of King Evelake. It took Beaufils several minutes to catch up with his friend, but when he did, Galahad smiled delightedly at him. "I *knew* that this adventure would be ours after all. We seek the Holy Grail, brought to this land by Joseph of Arimathea, so of course we should have the shield of Joseph of Arimathea's son. God has provided for us again on our quest!"

Beaufils didn't bother answering. When Galahad talked fervently about God, he never noticed what anyone else said anyway. Beaufils was busy watching for hidden attackers. Ten minutes later, Galahad spied the shield, hung in the fork of a tree just off the path, and Beaufils spotted what he was looking for: a man crouching atop a boulder above the forest track. "Why don't you say one more prayer before you go get the shield?" Beaufils suggested, sliding off his mule and slipping into the forest. He circled around behind the boulder, then climbed noiselessly up behind the man. Galahad had finished his prayer and was just about to ride past the stone, his eyes fixed on the shield. The waiting man stood up, holding high in both hands a rock the size of a man's head. Beaufils stepped up behind the man and, grasping the stone just as the man began to throw it, held it in place. The man released the stone, and Beaufils allowed it to drop with a dull thunk onto the man's head. The man crumpled in a heap. Beaufils made sure that the man wasn't seriously hurt, stretched him out in a comfortable position, then searched him. Sure enough,

Sir Brandegoris's money pouch was in the man's belt, so Beaufils took it and went back to Clover.

"Did you see, Beaufils?" Galahad asked. "The shield came away in my hands as easily as the sword came from the stone!"

"And now you have a shield, just as you wanted," Beaufils said.

"I must go back and thank the good priest who gave me absolution before this great trial," Galahad declared.

Beaufils looked thoughtfully at his companion. For himself, he was convinced that the priest was little more than a clever bandit, sending knights into a trap, where another man waited to bash them and steal their money, but it struck Beaufils suddenly that he shouldn't tell this to Galahad. Galahad regarded all priests as holy and blameless, and he'd never believe different. Beaufils shrugged and turned Clover back down the path after Galahad. He had to return Sir Brandegoris's money anyway.

On the fourth evening after they left Camelot, they came to what was by then their fifth church. This one was built of stone and looked older than the others they'd been to, and there were smaller slabs of carved stone scattered about the yard beside the church. At Beaufils's query, Galahad explained that those were graves, and while Galahad went in to see the priest,

Beaufils strolled among the gravestones, understanding for the first time why his mother had told him to bury her body and then cover the burial place with stones. It hadn't been just an odd idea of his mother's; it was an established custom among people. Of course it was still odd, but when everyone does the same odd thing, it seems almost normal.

Beaufils was used to Galahad taking at least an hour for a confession, but he had been in the graveyard barely ten minutes when Galahad reappeared, accompanied by a priest.

"Here it is, Sir Knight!" the priest was saying breathlessly. "This grave right here. Since the children first heard the noises, no one from the village will enter the churchyard. Some won't even come to church. I've heard the sounds myself, after dark, and they drove fear into my heart. O Sir Knight, if this is indeed a spirit from below, do not face it unless you are truly pure of heart!"

"If I am not, then I can never achieve the quest I have undertaken, and it would be better for me to die anyway," Galahad replied. "Leave me now, and I shall pray while I await this visitation."

The priest agreed readily and hurried back into the church. Beaufils watched him run, then asked, "What's the matter here?"

"You had best leave me, Beaufils," Galahad said. "The people of this town have heard the sounds of a foul spirit coming from this grave, as if the soul is unclean and should not have been buried in holy ground. I have vowed to face it and drive it away if I am able."

"That was kind of you," Beaufils said. "I'll stay with you while you wait."

Galahad didn't seem to hear. He had sunk to his knees and was already deep in fervent prayer. While Galahad whispered to himself, Beaufils examined the grave. This one was more elaborate than most, being covered with a long, flat, carved slab of stone. The carvings were words, but while Beaufils could sound them out, they weren't words he knew. If a spirit did come out of the grave, maybe he could ask it what they meant.

Less than an hour later, just as the sun was about to disappear in the west, there came a scratching and a huffing sound from inside the grave. Galahad began to pray more loudly and his breath came in gasps, as if he had been running a great distance. The sound stopped, then resumed, and Galahad fainted.

He just crumpled and fell forward, bumping his forehead against the headstone. Pulling him away from the grave, Beaufils found that Galahad was panting and perspiring and moaning just as he had the night when Beaufils had met Scotus. Beaufils waited a moment until the scratching began again, then took hold of one end of the great stone slab and pulled it away from the grave. The scratching stopped. Beaufils lowered his head into the dark hole he had opened and said, "Hello? Anyone home?"

As his eyes adjusted to the dark, Beaufils saw that the grave was not very deep, and in the faint moonlight even made out a few bones, scattered about, as if they'd been disturbed. Small piles of brush dotted the open hole. Just below the headstone Beaufils made out a second hole, round and about a hand's breadth wide. From this hole, two bright eyes peered out. Beaufils grinned. "Hello, dear," he said. He lowered his hand into the grave and waited expectantly. After a minute a hedgehog appeared from the round opening and sniffed Beaufils's hand tentatively. "You've been scaring the people around here," Beaufils said sternly. "Let's go find you another place to build a den." He carefully picked up the spiny creature and drew it from the hole, but as he lifted it out of the grave, Galahad moaned, and the hedgehog jumped from his hand and scurried back into its tunnel. Beaufils sighed. He had known many small animals when he was growing up, and he knew he'd not coax this one out again. For the next twenty minutes, Beaufils worked to plug up the hedgehog's tunnel with large stones. Then he pushed the slab back into place and waited for Galahad to awake from his swoon.

It was an hour before Galahad jerked into consciousness. "Did you see it?" he demanded.

"Yes, yes, I saw it," Beaufils said soothingly.

"What did it look like?" Galahad asked.

"Um, it had sharp points sticking out all over it," Beaufils replied carefully.

"Did it have a human shape?"

"No, not at all."

"Did it see me?" Galahad asked, his voice tense.

"Yes."

"What did it do?"

"It ran away. It was afraid of you, you see."

"Afraid of me!" Galahad repeated, wonder in his voice. "Then it is true! I truly am the purest of all knights! Even the spirits flee from me!"

Beaufils considered his friend in silence for a minute. He could tell him the truth, of course, but once again Beaufils knew instinctively that the truth would not be welcome. Galahad was so sure of his own way of seeing things that he wasn't really very interested in seeing anything that didn't fit. Beaufils realized with surprise that as much as he liked Galahad and respected him for his desire to do right, he was growing weary of his friend. You had to pretend too much when you were with Galahad, and it was starting to get tiresome.

V

THE CARL OF CARLISLE

Since leaving Camelot, Beaufils and Galahad had been traveling in a general northerly direction, varying their course only when Galahad got word of a church he could visit. On their sixth day out, Galahad told Beaufils that they were nearing Scotland and would enter that land soon after they passed through the town of Carlisle. All places were new to Beaufils, of course, so he didn't care one way or the other, but Galahad liked to tell him where they were, and Beaufils didn't mind hearing it.

On the outskirts of Carlisle, Beaufils had a new and wonderful experience—the delight of meeting an old friend. Crossing a field, they came upon Gawain, whom Beaufils greeted with pleasure. He was less excited to see that Gawain was accompanied by Bishop Baldwin from Camelot, but Galahad seemed more excited to encounter Bishop Baldwin, so it worked out very evenly.

As they rode into town, Beaufils fell back beside Gawain and gestured at Galahad and Bishop Baldwin riding ahead of them. "Galahad seems very pleased with Bishop Baldwin, doesn't he? Normally he only gets this excited about meeting priests."

Gawain glanced at him curiously. "Well, you know— or, rather, I suppose you don't—a bishop is a kind of priest."

"Oh, that explains it," Beaufils said. "I didn't know. I thought 'Bishop' was just a part of his name."

"No, it's a title," Gawain explained, "like king or duke or baron."

"Does everyone have a title?" Beaufils asked.

"No," Gawain replied. "It's a special privilege, and the people who have a title sometimes think it makes them very special indeed."

Beaufils smiled at Gawain's witticism. He had to be joking, of course; Beaufils knew that people would never really think they were special just because of extra words tacked onto their name. Changing the subject, Beaufils asked, "What brings you and Bishop Baldwin to Carlisle? Have you heard anything of that Grail thing we're looking for?"

Gawain shook his head. "Nay. I have no notion which way to look, so I thought I'd look up north. I have family in this direction, you see. It seemed like a good time to drop in for a visit. Why shouldn't the Grail be at my brother's house, after all? As for Baldwin"—his voice changed slightly, and Beaufils sensed Gawain's dislike of the priest—"I've no idea why he came this way. I found him lost on the moors yesterday. He'd been two days without food, so I fed him and brought him along. I thought I might drop him off with some wealthy patron here in Carlisle."

Beaufils asked what a wealthy patron was, and Gawain explained that sometimes noblemen—those people with extra words in their name—took care of priests. "I see," Beaufils said. "And have you found one?"

"Not yet," Gawain said, "but a villager on the road told me there's a castle up ahead that belongs to the Carl of Carlisle."

"Ah, and is 'Carl' another one of those titles?"

"Not usually," Gawain replied. "More often, it means a rough and boorish person, like 'churl,' but the villager told me that he owns most of the lands hereabouts, so I thought we'd give it a try. When he hears that we're from Arthur's court, he might put us all up for the night. These rich fellows often do."

Twenty minutes later, having asked for directions in town, the four came to the castle of the Carl of Carlisle. Gawain knocked on the great gate; then they waited. Nothing happened. No one opened the gate or even looked over the wall. Bishop Baldwin began to frown. "Try again!" he commanded Gawain.

Gawain cast the bishop a look of distaste, but he did as told and knocked again, harder. Again they waited in silence. Just before Gawain knocked a third time, the gate began to creak, and opened a crack. A slouching man in stained clothes peeked around the edge of the door. "What?" he demanded in a surly voice.

"Pardon our—" Gawain began.

"Open this gate at once," Bishop Baldwin commanded. "I am Bishop Baldwin of Camelot, and my escort includes two of knights of the Round Table! Tell your master we demand his hospitality for the night!"

"Baldwin," Gawain expostulated. "You can't—"

"I'll tell him," drawled the stained man, "and he might even let you stay, if he's in the mood, but I'll tell you now you'd rather not. Whyn't you go find a nice clean farmhouse somewhere?"

"We are from Camelot," Bishop Baldwin replied, "and we do not sleep in farmhouses."

"We don't?" Beaufils asked Gawain. "Why not? Is there a rule?"

"I've slept in many a farmhouse and been glad for it," Gawain said quietly to Beaufils. "Better than the woods, I say."

"All right," the man at the gate said. "I'll tell the Carl. You come on in if you're minded, but don't say I didn't warn you." With that he pushed the gate open wider and shuffled away.

The four travelers rode into the filthiest place that Beaufils had ever seen. The castle courtyard was strewn with all sorts of stinking piles of garbage and rotting food. Rats scampered about in the open, and swarms of flies filled the air. "You want to rethink the farmhouse idea?" Gawain asked, but Bishop Baldwin either didn't hear or pretended not to. No one dismounted while they waited in the courtyard for the doorman to return; no one wanted to step in something nasty.

At last the stained man leaned from the window and said, "The Carl says to suit yourselves. Stay here if you want; it's no skin off his arse."

He turned away, but before he disappeared inside again, Gawain called out, "And, sir, forgive me, but is there a place we can put our horses?"

"If you want, you can leave 'em with the asses in the stable," the man said with a grunt, gesturing to a ramshackle building against the far wall.

"Thank you," Gawain said, bowing politely.

Having seen the piles of ordure in the courtyard, Beaufils was not surprised to find the stables filled with dung, but there was plenty of hay as well. Beaufils dismounted and, taking up a rusty shovel that leaned against one wall, began moving the piles of manure aside so that they could bring their mounts in. It was a long stable, with many separate stalls, each one occupied by a fat donkey. This circumstance seemed to bother Galahad and Bishop Baldwin even more than the smell of the manure.

"I'm not leaving my horse in a stall with an ass!" Bishop Baldwin said abruptly.

"Indeed, it is hardly appropriate," agreed Galahad.

Beaufils didn't know why they were concerned; the stalls were all large enough for two animals, or even three. He didn't ask for an explanation, though; he was busy. Working quickly with his shovel, he mucked out a stall; then he led Clover in to meet his new donkey friend. He had just finished rubbing down the mule and was petting the silken forehead of the donkey when he heard a commotion nearby. Looking out, he saw Bishop Baldwin pushing and shoving a very determined little donkey out of the next stall. The animal's legs were locked, and its head lowered stubbornly as Bishop Baldwin shoved at its hindquarters.

"What are you doing?" Beaufils asked.

The bishop didn't reply at once, his face red with exertion, but after pushing for a while longer, he said, "I'm moving this ass out of my horse's stall, clodpate! What does it look like I'm doing?"

"It looks like you're shoving at his bottom and moving him nowhere," Beaufils replied. "Why do you want him to move?"

"My horse is a blood stallion. I won't have him sharing a stall with a lowly beast like that!"

Beaufils clucked to the donkey and scratched its head. "You can't help how tall you are, can you, dear?" He looked up at the bishop. "Where do you want the donkey?"

"I don't care. Anywhere but here!"

"Let's see if your neighbor would like company," Beaufils said, leading the donkey to the next stall.

"Well, that's done then," Bishop Baldwin said, brushing himself off with satisfaction as if he had accomplished something. "Shall we go meet our churlish host?"

Gawain, who had been leaning against the stable wall watching the bishop's ineffective labors, said, "If Galahad's ready."

Galahad joined them a moment later. He, too, had been delayed by the need to remove a donkey from his horse's stall, but he had accomplished this task on his own by the simple expedient of stretching both arms under the donkey's belly and carrying it to the next stall. When the men were together, they picked their way out of the stable, through the filthy courtyard, and into the central tower of the castle.

There they were met by the dirty doorman, who jerked his head down a corridor. "Carl says you can have the east guest hall, if you like. Or if you don't. It's down there, end of the hall." Then he meandered off, leaving the four to find their own way.

The guest hall was much like the rest of the castle: filthy and crawling with animals. Scrawny chickens pecked their way around the room, mice scurried everywhere, and several large dogs lay in the floor blocking their path. One of these, just as they entered, raised one leg and released a loud explosion of gas. "Figures," said Gawain, stepping over the dog and looking about at the cobwebby chairs. From the hall itself, several doors opened into smaller rooms, where Beaufils could make out some filthy beds. "Maybe I'll go sleep in the stable with a donkey," Gawain added.

A squirrel chattered at them from the rafters and threw a nut down, which bounced harmlessly off Galahad's armor. Beaufils glanced at the squirrel, noted a line of bats clinging to the ceiling, and said, "It seems that the Carl likes animals."

"More than he likes visitors, anyway," replied Gawain. "I'm beginning to have my doubts about our being invited to dinner with our gracious host."

But Gawain's doubts were unfounded. After they had each chosen a bedchamber and dusted off their beds as well as they could (though not without some complaining from Bishop Baldwin and Galahad), the surly doorman strolled into the room without knocking and said, "Carl says if you want to eat, you can come sit at table with him. Don't if you don't want to, though. No skin off his—"

"Yes, yes, we know," Gawain said. "We'll be with him at once. Which way?"

The man led them through cluttered corridors to a huge banquet hall, littered with the debris of past meals, and Beaufils got his first look at the Carl of Carlisle.

The man was huge—unnaturally so, in fact—for he must have stood a head taller than Gawain, who towered above the rest of them. He also seemed to be twice as broad as Gawain and at least three times as hairy. The Carl's thick black hair jutted out in long greasy tufts from his head, and his beard looked like a bearskin across his great chest. All four travelers stopped at the door and stared. The Carl gave them a cursory glance.

"Well, don't stand there gawking like great gabies," he said in a booming voice. "Food's on the table." Silently, they moved toward the long table, but before they could sit, the Carl spoke again, to Galahad and Beaufils. "Not in those two chairs, ye bufflebutts. Those're for my wife and daughter."

"I'm sorry," Beaufils replied. "I didn't know. Is that chair across the table all right?"

"Suit yourself," the Carl grunted.

At least the food looks good, Beaufils thought as he walked around the table and took his seat. Growing up

with his mother in the forest, he had eaten mostly vegetables and nuts, and King Arthur's banquet, which
had consisted largely of roasted meats, had not tasted
very good to him. He had, however, loved the king's
bread, and so he was pleased to see that the Carl's dinner was made up entirely of brown bread. His companions were clearly less pleased, though. Beaufils heard
Bishop Baldwin mutter something about "paltry fare,"
and even Gawain seemed disappointed with the food.

A few minutes after they began eating, the door opened
and two women entered, and all four of the travelers
stopped eating to stare at them, because it would have
been impossible to imagine two women more ill-suited
to their surroundings. One of the women looked older
than the other—Beaufils guessed that these were the
Carl's wife and daughter—but both looked clean and
fresh and pleasant. They smiled at the travelers
and greeted them warmly, then sat beside the Carl and
began to eat. The Carl, his mouth stuffed full of food,
said something to them under his breath, wiped his
mouth with the back of his hand, and tossed a crust of
bread over his shoulder.

Gawain introduced himself and his three companions to the women, then made polite conversation while
they ate. Listening, Beaufils learned that the older
woman's name was Elspeth and the younger was called
Ellyn. Beaufils didn't join the conversation, though,

neither did Galahad or Bishop Baldwin. This puzzled Beaufils, since he had not noticed Bishop Baldwin being reluctant to speak before, but their silence was explained after dinner, when the four were back in the guest hall.

"Now it all becomes clear!" Galahad announced as soon as they were alone. "This is a place of temptation, a test for us on our quest for the Holy Grail!"

Gawain glanced around their squalid quarters. "You find something tempting in here?"

"Not here! Those women of such beauty! The filth and the stench of the castle are a warning to us against temptation! We must leave at once!"

Gawain frowned at Galahad. "I don't mind leaving, but I must say that I think you're misjudging Lady Elspeth and Lady Ellyn."

"The good knight Sir Galahad is right!" Bishop Baldwin said. "Can you deny, Sir Gawain, that those two women of such unearthly beauty of form and face and figure can hardly be of this world? They are here to test our virtue."

"Nonsense," Gawain said, his voice rising slightly. Before he could continue, though, a gentle tapping came from the door. Beaufils opened it to see the Carl's daughter Ellyn standing there. "Oh, hello," he said to her. "We were just talking about you. Come in."

"Good evening," Ellyn said, stepping into the room,

bringing a scent of flowers with her. "I just came to see if there was anything else you wanted before you went to bed."

"See?" Galahad said, his voice cracking slightly. "I told you so!"

"Yes, Sir Galahad?" Ellyn asked, her brow wrinkling slightly in confusion. "Did you want something?"

"I want nothing from you."

Ellyn looked surprised at Galahad's vehemence. She replied rigidly but politely, "Very well."

"Galahad, don't be an ass," Gawain said.

Galahad ignored him, speaking again to Ellyn. "Come no closer. I will not give in." Then Galahad closed his eyes tightly.

Gawain sighed. After a moment Ellyn said, "If you're all right, then, I'll leave you now." She turned and left the room, and Beaufils, after giving Galahad another glance, followed her into the hallway and closed the door behind him.

"Sorry about that," he said. "I'm afraid my friend was a bit rude."

"What was he talking about?" Ellyn asked.

"I don't really know," Beaufils said. "Galahad sometimes gets ideas that I don't understand. All I know is there's no use trying to talk him out of them."

Ellyn looked at Beaufils curiously. "But he's your friend, you say?"

"Oh, yes," Beaufils said. They began walking together down the hall. "He always does what he thinks is right, and you have to admire that about him. I've begun to realize that's not very common among men."

Ellyn gave a snort. "If you've only just begun to realize that, you must have lived a sheltered life until now."

Beaufils smiled. "I have. In fact, until a few weeks ago, I'd never met another human being other than my mother."

"You're joking!" Ellyn said, her eyes wide. "How could that be?"

For the next two hours, Beaufils told her. They walked together down the hall as he talked, then up a long stairway to the top of a tower. There they sat together, above the smell of decay that filled the castle below, while Beaufils told Ellyn about his mother and his early life, then finally about his experiences since leaving the forest. Ellyn told Beaufils nothing about herself, but she asked many questions and clearly enjoyed his story very much.

"You *have* been through it since leaving home, haven't you?" she said when he was done. "All the worst sorts of people—bandits and renegade priests and all that."

"It's very strange, though," Beaufils admitted. "It all seems to come from people wanting things they don't need, just because someone else has them."

Ellyn nodded slowly. "Indeed, you're right. People

always want to possess whatever other people want. It's been the bane of my life since I became a woman."

"What do you mean?"

"Well," Ellyn replied gloomily, "a lot of people seem to think that I'm very pretty. This sounds like a good thing, but it's not. When men think a girl is pretty, they seem to think that's all she is. Everywhere I go, men either fall all over themselves to catch my attention, or take me in immediate dislike, like your friend Galahad. Either way, it's never about me but only about my appearance. It puts you off people, I can tell you. I can't think of one person, apart from my parents, I'd put myself to any trouble for."

Beaufils shook his head with wonder. "You need to meet more people. I've met *lots* of people I'd be happy to help if I could. After all, they're usually so nice to me."

Ellyn looked at him wryly. "You think so? Like those girls at Camelot who followed you around?"

"Well, yes. It was very kind of them to be so nice to a stranger."

Ellyn snorted again. "See how nice they are to a stranger with a mole on his nose. You poor innocent. They were following you because you are an incredibly beautiful young man. Girls who see you are going to become silly, giggly, blushing, simpering widgeons, just like men who see me all seem to become silly, strutting, boastful, peacocky nitwits."

"But you didn't blush and giggle when you met me," Beaufils pointed out.

"And you didn't strut and boast when you met me," Ellyn replied. "I can't tell you how nice it was, too."

Beaufils grinned. "Does this mean we can be friends?"

Ellyn returned his smile. "I guess so. But what will your friend Galahad think?"

"I don't know," Beaufils replied frankly. "But you mustn't be hurt by Galahad's talk. It wasn't about you in particular. I think he's afraid of all women." Beaufils was remembering what the old man, Scotus, had told him about Galahad's dream.

A voice rang out below them in the courtyard, and Ellyn looked over the edge of the tower. "Well, I suppose we can find out now. There's your friend Galahad, and he's calling for you."

Together they descended the tower and made their way to the courtyard, where they found Galahad and Bishop Baldwin, already mounted and leading Clover.

"There you are!" Galahad exclaimed when Beaufils stepped out of the tower. "Come! We must leave this—" He broke off when Ellyn stepped out the door behind Beaufils. "I see," Galahad said, his voice scornful. "No wonder we couldn't find you. Have you been with this woman all evening?"

"Yes. She's my friend," Beaufils replied. "Are we leaving?"

"Some of us are," Galahad said, his voice cold. "Where's Gawain?"

"He has chosen to remain," Bishop Baldwin said. "In his pride, he believes he can withstand temptation."

"More like doesn't believe there's any temptation to withstand," growled Gawain from the doorway. He stepped forward and looked at Beaufils. "There you are, lad. Don't listen to Baldwin. I told them I wouldn't sneak out of a castle in the middle of the night without taking leave of my hosts, and that's why I'm staying. Hello, my lady."

"Good evening, Sir Gawain," replied Ellyn.

"O'erweening pride!" pronounced Bishop Baldwin.

"What does that mean?" asked Beaufils.

"Don't worry about it, lad," replied Gawain. "Baldwin doesn't know, either."

"Beaufils," said Galahad suddenly. "You have been a good companion to me, and one who has fought spiritual battles by my side. I will allow you to ride away with us if you agree to find the nearest church and confess your sins."

Beaufils pondered this for a moment. He wasn't sure what sins Galahad thought he had to confess, and he was about to ask when Gawain spoke for him. "And if not?"

"Then we part ways at once!" Galahad said in a ringing voice. "He may stay with you if he so chooses!"

"Oh, may I?" Beaufils asked Gawain. "I think I'd like that."

"I would too, lad," Gawain said.

"You have chosen your path, and may you live to regret it."

"Er . . . thank you," Beaufils said. "I hope you live, too."

Galahad turned his horse with a sharp tug on his reins, but at that moment a huge black shadow appeared between the two riders and the castle gate. "What's all this noise in the middle of the night!" rumbled a deep voice. It was the Carl himself.

Bishop Baldwin's eyes widened, and he drew back from the Carl, but Galahad turned to face the Carl squarely. "We are leaving this castle of temptations at once!" he declared.

"Over my dead body or not at all!" the Carl said. "If you want to leave, you'll have to kill me."

"What?" gasped Galahad.

"Go on!" the Carl said. "Cut off my head if you're man enough! I won't stop you."

Beaufils glanced at Ellyn, who was watching her father calmly. Beaufils didn't understand this last bit at all.

"Go on, little girls!" the Carl snapped. "Draw your swords! Hit me if you dare!"

"Do it, Galahad!" said Bishop Baldwin. "Kill him before he kills us!"

Galahad grasped his sword, drew it partly from its scabbard, then thrust it back in. "No!" he called. "It's another temptation! He wants me to commit the sin of wrath! A mortal sin!"

"Well, go ahead and do it now, and then you can confess later! I'll hear your confession myself," Bishop Baldwin replied.

"No!" screamed Galahad, after which he booted his horse into a gallop and raced through the courtyard to the front gate.

Bishop Baldwin took one look at the Carl, squawked "Wait for me!," then followed. A minute later he and Galahad were gone.

"Damn," said the Carl.

"Do you mind explaining what that was about?" Gawain asked the Carl calmly.

The Carl shook his head and, turning away, stomped back into the castle.

Ellyn smiled at Beaufils. "Good night, Beaufils. Good night, Sir Gawain. Will you be leaving in the morning?"

"Ay, I suppose so," Gawain said. "But look here, my lady, what was your father up to, demanding that—?"

"Then I'll see you tomorrow," she said, following her father into the castle.

The next morning, Gawain and Beaufils rose at dawn and saddled their mounts in preparation for leaving. When all was ready, Gawain said, "Come on, Le Beau, let's go look for our puzzling host and his family."

They didn't have to look far. When they stepped out of the stable, there was the Carl, with his wife and daughter on either side.

"Leaving?" the Carl growled.

"We are, sir," Gawain replied calmly. "But not without taking our leave of you. We thank you, sir, for your hospitality."

"You've nothing to thank me for," the Carl snapped. "I've put myself to no trouble for you."

"Well, that's true, at any rate," Gawain agreed. "We've slept on dirty beds and eaten old, dry bread. But whether or not you've been a model host, I've still been your guest, and I thank you."

The Carl looked down at Gawain, his eyes speculative. "Mighty pretty manners," he grunted at last. "Maybe I should follow your example. Sir Gawain, would you do me one favor?"

"If it is within my power, yes, I will," Gawain replied promptly.

"Oh, it's within your power," the Carl said. With that, he knelt before Gawain. "Cut my head off."

Gawain stared at the Carl, then looked at the two women. They were watching the scene calmly. "Cut your head off?" Gawain repeated.

"Ay. Cut it off," the Carl replied.

"Is that good manners?" Beaufils asked, puzzled.

"Not as a rule, lad, no," Gawain said. He knelt before the Carl and said, "Actually, I'd rather not, sir."

"You said you'd do it if you were able," the Carl snapped with a frown. "Are ye a man of your word or not?"

"Is this what you want?" Gawain asked again.

"Why would I ask it if I didn't want it?" the Carl said. "Is it the sort of thing a man'd be likely to joke about?"

Gawain stood and looked at Elspeth and Ellyn. "My ladies? Is this *your* wish?"

Neither lady replied. They simply looked at Gawain, showing nothing.

"What do you think, Le Beau?" Gawain asked.

"I'm not the one who's been asked," Beaufils replied. "I think it'd better be your own decision."

Gawain looked at the kneeling Carl for a moment, then said, "I do not take beheading lightly. By a careless blow I once brought on myself the greatest shame of my life." He thought for a moment. "But by another such blow I brought myself my greatest honor. All right, O Carl. I will keep my promise." Then Gawain drew his sword, and with one swift motion brought it down on the back of the Carl's neck.

There was a great crash, like thunder, and a white mist began drifting up from the piles of refuse that lay on every side. In seconds, Beaufils could see nothing but the thick fog before his eyes. Then his right cheek felt a faint chill, and a breeze began to blow away the fog. When the mist was completely gone, Beaufils stared around himself with delight. It was as if the wind had blown him to a different castle. Gone were the piles of garbage, gone was the reek of decay. Everything was spotless, and at his feet, groaning and gingerly touching his neck, knelt a slender man with a neatly trimmed black beard.

"Father?" whispered Ellyn.

"Here, Ellyn," the man said. Both women knelt beside the man and embraced him, weeping.

Beaufils glanced at Gawain. "This isn't what usually happens when you cut off someone's head, is it?"

Gawain grinned. "Hardly."

"Good," Beaufils said, relieved. "I was afraid that I had a whole lot more to learn about the world than I thought."

The Carl stood and stretched out both arms to Sir Gawain. "Thank you, Sir Gawain. You have released me from a great enchantment."

"That much I had figured out," Gawain said, returning the embrace. "Do you mind telling me about it?"

"I used to be called the Earl of Carlisle," the Carl began. They were all back in the great banquet hall, eating a hot breakfast together. "I was the wealthiest man and the greatest nobleman in these parts, which at the time seemed very important to me. I grew very vain, I'm afraid."

"You did, a bit," said his wife, Elspeth, "though never to your own family and friends. It was how I knew that you really weren't as pompous as you sometimes seemed."

"At any rate, I was pompous once too often," the Carl said. "I treated a poor old vagabond as if he were nothing. He came to ask for a bit of food for the road, and I tossed him a crust of day-old brown bread and told him to be gone." The Carl reddened at the memory, then went on. "Anyway, it turned out this vagabond was a magician or sorcerer, and he laid a spell on me. I became a monster, and my home became . . . well, you saw what it was like. My great horses became asses, my servants became slovenly oafs, and no matter what was served at my table, it immediately became day-old brown bread."

"I rather liked the bread," Beaufils commented.

"But Elspeth and Ellyn? They weren't transformed," Gawain pointed out.

"That's because they had been kind to the old

enchanter. In fact, they were the ones who sent him to the castle to get food. They had met him on the road when they were out riding."

"He seemed a nice old gentleman," Ellyn said. "His name was Scotus."

Beaufils caught his breath but kept his face still and his eyes lowered. His old man was an enchanter?

"Scotus, eh?" said Gawain.

"Do you know him?"

"I know an enchanter with a name something like that," Gawain replied. "But go on with your story. What was all this about cutting your head off?"

"The enchanter said that I could only be restored to the person I was supposed to be if I humbled myself to the point of death. Beheading just seemed like the surest way to do that. The only other thing that he added was that neither I nor anyone else could tell anyone about my enchantment."

Ellyn smiled ruefully at Beaufils. "You can't know how hard it was for me to keep my tongue when we were talking last night. You told me so freely about your own life; I felt horribly ungrateful not telling you anything about myself."

"But now you can tell me anything you want, right?" Beaufils said.

"I could," Ellyn said. "But you and Sir Gawain are leaving now."

Beaufils shrugged. "Why don't you come with us? You don't mind, do you Gawain?"

Gawain grinned. "*I* don't, but Ellyn and her family may have other plans."

Ellyn's mouth opened in a perfect little oval, and her eyes lit up. "Do you really mean it? Oh, Father, Mother! Do you mind?"

"You *want* to go adventuring?" Elspeth asked her daughter. "Now that everything's finally restored at home?"

"I *couldn't* have gone off with Father under the spell," Ellyn explained. "That would have been deserting him. But now, oh it would be the most wonderful adventure! And with Beaufils and Sir Gawain, too, the only two men I've ever met who don't act silly around me just because I'm pretty."

The Carl—he forbade anyone to call him "Earl," saying that "Carl" was good enough for him now—and Elspeth needed to be coaxed a bit more, but in the end it was three riders who set off together to seek the Grail: a formidable middle-aged knight, a beautiful maiden, and Beaufils. Beaufils could not help smiling in anticipation; he was sure this was going to be fun.

VI

HOLY MEN LIKE FLEAS

"Why do you call Beaufils 'Le Beau,' Sir Gawain?" asked Ellyn. They were following a thin track across a moor toward the dark line of trees that marked the edge of a forest.

"You can just call me Gawain, Lady Ellyn," the knight replied. "You don't have to use the formal title while we travel."

"Thank you, and you can call me just Ellyn, but I was asking about what you call Beaufils."

Gawain grinned and glanced at Beaufils. "You want to tell her?"

"If you like," Beaufils replied. He looked at Ellyn and said, "You see, I'm not sure if Beaufils is even my real name. It was what my mother always called me, but it turns out that it's just another way of saying 'fair son.'"

"You don't even know if it's your real name? Didn't your mother ever call you anything else?"

"Why would she?" Beaufils replied. "Without any other people around, we always knew who we were talking to. Until a few weeks ago, I didn't even know that people had their own special names."

"Anyway," Gawain said, "when our friend here came to Camelot and explained all this, a friend of mine there—Sir Kai—called him 'Le Beau Desconus,' which means something like 'the Fair Unknown.' I just like the sound of that better than 'Fair Son.' "

"I think I do, too," Ellyn said. "After all, you're not just somebody's fair son; you're more than that."

"But what?" Beaufils asked.

"That," Ellyn replied, "is still unknown, isn't it?"

They had come to the edge of the forest by now, and their narrow path led right into the thick trees. Beaufils's eye was caught by an unexpected gleam of white beside the track, and looking more closely, he made out a small painted sign, nearly hidden by several years' growth of saplings. The faded letters of the sign read THE SACRED FOREST.

"What the devil does that mean?" Gawain asked, after Beaufils had pointed it out to the others.

"I've heard stories of *enchanted* forests," Ellyn remarked. "I'm not sure what a sacred forest is, though."

"I would have thought all forests were sacred," Beaufils added.

"Anyway, it sounds promising," Gawain said. "Where better to look for a Holy Grail than in a sacred forest?"

The passage between the trees was tight enough that they had to ride single file. Gawain went first, followed by Ellyn, and Beaufils brought up the rear. It was hard to carry on a conversation that way, and Beaufils hoped that the path through the sacred forest wouldn't always be so narrow. Thus he was pleased when, just a few minutes after they entered the woods, the path widened and emptied into a small clearing. There he saw a tiny one-room log house with a very old, obviously long unused cookfire outside.

"What a small house," Beaufils commented. "Even the house that Mother and I made in our forest was bigger than that."

"Looks like a hermitage to me," Gawain said.

"What's that?"

"It's where a hermit lives," Gawain said. Then, at Beaufils's puzzled frown, Gawain chuckled. "I'll have to do better than that, won't I? Let's see. A hermit is a person who goes off to live alone and think about God. That probably doesn't make sense, does it?"

Beaufils frowned and said slowly, "No, I think I understand. I've only been in the world outside our forest a short time now, but I can see that it might be easier to think about God when you're alone. The world's a bit loud, isn't it? So these hermits are very holy men?"

Gawain avoided Beaufils's eyes as he replied, "Er, I *have* met one who was, yes."

Beaufils smiled. "Then I should like to meet a hermit. Pity that this hermitage is empty."

"Just what I was thinking," Gawain said. "Oh well, I suppose we should move on."

Before long, they came to another empty hermitage, and then a third. Ellyn said she was beginning to have an idea why this was called the Sacred Forest.

At last, at their fourth hermitage, they had better luck and found a real hermit, although Gawain managed to conceal his pleasure. The hermit was a tall, stoop-shouldered man with black hair that was turning gray at the sides. As the travelers rode into his clearing, the hermit rose to his feet and said, "I bid you welcome, travelers, if you are friends of God," the man said.

"Well, I think we are," Gawain said. "I'm Sir Gawain of Orkney, and this is Lady Ellyn of Carlisle and Le Beau of Desconus. We are on a quest together in this forest."

The hermit's eyes had grown suddenly intent. "What do you mean, you *think* you are friends of God?" he demanded.

Gawain blinked but replied, "I just meant that we try to be."

The man shook his head vigorously. "Then you are greatly misled. You can never be God's friend by trying, can never be justified by your own efforts. You must realize that you are sinners to the core."

"Oh," Gawain said. "Do you, ah, do you know us, sir?"

"Do not take my words personally," the hermit said. "I speak not only of you but of all humanity. I know of what I speak; I am Father Rolbert, formerly master of theology at Oxford University."

"Formerly?" Gawain asked, glancing around at Father Rolbert's spare hermit's quarters.

"I could not stay at Oxford, for my soul's sake. You may not believe this, but even in that place of divine study, I found false doctrine and heresy. I could no longer associate with false teachers. The truth is not in them." His eyes glowed unpleasantly, and Beaufils felt mildly disappointed. He wasn't sure what very holy men were like, but he hadn't imagined they would be like this.

Gawain nodded slowly. "I'll keep that in mind. Listen, Father Rolbert, what we are really seeking is something called the Holy Grail."

"If you are destined to find it, then you shall. If not, then you can never do so."

"Just like that?" asked Gawain. "All a matter of destiny?"

"That is correct," Father Rolbert said.

Gawain scratched his beard, then said, "But if that's true, then I don't have to look for the thing at all, do I? I mean, if I'm destined to find the Grail, then it'll come to me. I can just go back to court and drink beer and wait."

Father Rolbert shook his head, frowning. "No, if you did that, it would be a sure sign that you were *not* destined to achieve your quest."

"Then what I choose to do *does* make a difference," Gawain said.

"No, no. You have no choice at all. Just as God, in his mercy, has preordained some to heaven and some to eternal flames, so he has also preordained the one who will achieve this and every other quest."

"I'm confused," said Beaufils. "Should we keep looking for the Grail or not?"

"Yes, you should," Father Rolbert replied, with the air of one instructing a small and not particularly bright child. "But do not seek it because you think you can achieve it. You can achieve nothing of yourself. Instead, seek it because it might be God's will for you to find it."

This didn't really make any more sense to Beaufils, but he nodded politely, hoping to avoid any further explanations.

"How about this?" Gawain said. "Suppose for a moment that we might be fated to find the Grail—"

A spasm of distaste crossed Father Rolbert's face, and he interrupted hastily. "Not fated; predestined."

"What's the difference?" Gawain asked.

"Fate is the heresy that the pagan Greeks and Romans taught; predestination is the true doctrine of the right faith."

"Right, my mistake," Gawain said. "As I was about to say, if we *were* predestined to find the Grail, do you know which direction we might be predestined to take? I see that there are two different paths leaving this clearing."

"It matters little which way you take," Father Rolbert said, shaking his head sadly. "Both paths lead to grave danger."

"What sort of danger? Monsters? Recreant knights?"

"Worse! Down each of those paths is a hermit, both of whom teach heretical falsehoods that imperil your very soul. They are *not* of God's elect."

Beaufils grinned. "Recreant hermits?" he asked.

Gawain chuckled, then jerked his head at one of the paths. "Shall we take a chance on the doctrinal danger to the right? If you're not too frightened, I mean."

"I'm very brave," Ellyn said. "The righthand path it is." With that, the three companions rode away, leaving Father Rolbert alone again. Beaufils hoped that having correct doctrines was good company.

Ten minutes later they came to the next clearing and

drew up at the edge of the forest, watching. At first Beaufils thought this hermitage was deserted as well, but then he saw a tendril of smoke rising from a hole in the roof.

"Do we really want to do this?" Gawain asked.

"I was just wondering that, too," replied Ellyn.

"Seems like you can't fling a rock in this forest without beaning a holy man," Gawain added. "Not that I'm suggesting that, necessarily."

"They're as thick as fleas," agreed Ellyn.

Beaufils was puzzled. "You think this hermit might be like Father Rolbert?" Gawain and Ellyn nodded. "Why?" asked Beaufils. "There must be more than one kind of holiness, after all."

Gawain muttered, "Hope so," then bowed and gestured for Beaufils to go ahead of him. "As you wish, lad. Lead the way."

Beaufils urged Clover out of the trees and into the clearing, calling out, "Hello? Hermit?"

A smiling, yellow-haired man came to the door of the hut and waved. He looked to be about Gawain's age. "Welcome, travelers," he said.

"Thank you," Beaufils replied. Since he had gone first, he supposed that he was expected to speak for the group.

"I don't get many knights and ladies as visitors," the hermit replied, looking past Beaufils. "But you are welcome. I am Brother Denys."

"I'm glad to know you," Beaufils replied. "I'm Beaufils, and these are my friends Gawain and Ellyn."

"*Sir* Gawain? Of Arthur's court?" Brother Denys said, smiling widely. "I am honored. What brings you to my humble hermitage?"

Brother Denys still hadn't given Beaufils more than a cursory glance, addressing himself entirely to the others, but Beaufils continued to speak. "Actually, Brother Denys, we're on a quest. Some say it's a holy sort of quest, so we thought maybe a holy man could help us."

"A holy quest?" Brother Denys asked, finally looking at Beaufils.

"Yes," Beaufils replied. "We're looking for something called the Grail. It appeared to King Arthur's court a week or so back, floating in the air, and a loud voice came from nowhere saying that it was the goal of everyone's desire. Then it disappeared. Have you seen anything like that around here?"

Brother Denys's face lit up. "What a miracle! How I wish I had been there!"

"Does that mean yes or no?" Beaufils asked.

"I've seen nothing like that here, though I do see many visions."

"Bother," Beaufils said to his companions. "No luck here, either."

"Either?" asked Brother Denys, his voice sharper. "Whom else have you been asking?"

"Well, we just came from the hut of Father Rolbert—"

"Father Rolbert!" interrupted Brother Denys, with sudden sharpness. "Don't speak to me of Father Rolbert!"

"But you asked me who we had—"

"I never want to hear of Father Rolbert again! Father Rolbert's faith is all *head* faith! He knows how to divide syllogisms and talk the ears off a mule, but he has no *heart*! Father Rolbert wouldn't know a vision if it sat on his face! Father Rolbert has driven more good young men away from the faith than Satan himself. I hate the sound of his name!"

"Why do you keep saying it, then?" asked Beaufils.

"If you've been to see *him*," Brother Denys said, ignoring Beaufils's question, "then you are in grave danger of being led astray."

"Funny," commented Beaufils, "that's what he said about—"

"Come here, boy," Brother Denys said. He held out his arms, and Beaufils slipped obligingly from Clover's back and came to the hermit, who reached out and gripped both of Beaufils's hands in his own, then raised his eyes toward the sky. "Purge this boy of evil, I pray! Rid his mind of the dry doctrines of the devil! Enter his heart and warm it, O Spirit!"

Brother Denys went on like this for another few minutes, occasionally giving Beaufils's hands a squeeze, as if to show particular seriousness. Beaufils looked helplessly over his shoulder at Gawain and Ellyn. Ellyn looked concerned, but Gawain was grinning broadly. When he caught Beaufils's eyes, he wiggled his gauntleted fingers in a little wave.

Brother Denys prayed on. "Oh, remove sin and falseness from this boy's heart and mind, I pray, oh yes, oh yes, render us up in Thy sight, yes, and bind Satan from his attacks, yes, yes . . ." The hermit actually began to cry, tears rolling proudly down his cheeks. "Show us the true way of your Spirit!" he proclaimed. Then his eyes, pointed toward heaven, widened oddly.

Beaufils followed the hermit's gaze but saw nothing above them. "Is there something up there?" Beaufils asked.

Brother Denys, still crying, released Beaufils and raised his arms above his head. Beaufils stepped back quickly, to make sure he didn't get caught again, but the hermit wasn't watching him anymore. His lips moved, his eyes glazed over, and still he wept. At last he lowered his arms and focused his gaze on Beaufils. "Did you feel it?" he asked.

"Of course I felt it. You were squeezing me."

"Not that! The Spirit! Did you feel the Spirit fall on you? Did your heart warm? Did you cry?"

"Er, no," Beaufils said. Then, at the hermit's crestfallen look, added, "Sorry."

"We must try again!" the hermit announced. "You must try harder! Simply believe that it will happen, and it will! This time we'll pray in tongues!"

Beaufils leaped up on Clover's back. He had no idea what Brother Denys meant to do with his tongue, but Beaufils had had enough. "No, thank you," he said hastily. "The thing is, we're really looking for this Grail, and if you haven't seen one about, we should be moving on."

"I see what it is," Brother Denys said sternly. "Your heart is hardened!"

"Bad luck for me, I guess," Beaufils said, edging Clover away from the hermit. When he was well clear, he tapped the mule with his heel and trotted across the clearing to the place where the trail picked up again. A minute later Gawain and Ellyn joined him. Both were shaking with laughter. "You have to admit," Beaufils said, "that *was* a different sort of holiness than Father Rolbert's."

They continued on through the Sacred Forest, hard riding all the way. The trail was still so narrow that they had to move single file between the close trees and shrubbery. So thick was the undergrowth that Beaufils, still in the front position, didn't see the next clearing until it was a few yards ahead of him, which gave him no time to slow Clover's trot. The three companions burst from the trees into the clearing, almost at the same moment, and a black-robed man jumped up from a tree stump. "Is it you?" he shrieked.

Beaufils glanced uncertainly at the others, but they seemed as confused as he was, so he said, "I don't know about the others, but I'm certainly me, if that's what you mean."

"Are you the Four Horsemen?" the man shrieked. He pronounced his words oddly, rolling his "r" sounds in the back of his throat. Again the companions exchanged glances. Finally Ellyn said, "I don't think so, sir. You see, I'm not a horseman."

"And Clover here isn't a horse," Beaufils added.

"Plus, there are only three of us," said Gawain. "Besides that, you're pretty close, though."

The man in black seemed to relax. "Who are you then?" he demanded.

Gawain said, "I am Sir Gawain, and I am on quest with Lady Ellyn and Le Beau Desconus here. We are seeking a miraculous object called the Holy Grail."

"Le Beau Desconus?" the man said in his oddly accented speech. "The Beautiful Unknown?"

"Yes, actually," Gawain said. "You're French?"

"Yes. I am the Père d'Arbé, come to this place to await the coming millennium in prayer and penance."

"Millennium?" Beaufils asked. "What's that?"

Gawain winced and waved his hand sharply back and forth, clearly trying to stop Beaufils from asking, but it

119

was too late. The Père d'Arbé's eyes lit up, and he said, "It is the Thousand Year Reign that will follow the time of Great Tribulation and precede the End of All Things!"

"Oh," Beaufils said politely. "Thank you. I just hadn't heard—"

"And the time is near!" the Père d'Arbé went on. "I've just finished a chart, and when I looked at my calculations, I couldn't believe what I was seeing! Within this month, twice seventy weeks of years from Daniel's vision of Jeremiah's prophecy, the Beast will arise!"

"We'll keep our eyes open for it," Gawain said. "Look, we don't want to disturb you, but—"

"I had calculated the dates before," the hermit said, "but I had forgotten that in the time of John the Divine, years had only three hundred and sixty days. That's why I was mistaken six months ago. I admit that I was wrong. But this time, I'm *certain!*"

Gawain continued doggedly. "I'm sure you have other calculations to make, so we'll be leaving you now."

"Aren't we going to ask about the Grail?" Beaufils asked, surprised.

"Grail?" the Père d'Arbé asked. "What's that?"

Gawain waved his hand again but Beaufils said, "It's this platter, or bowl, that we're looking for. It appeared at King Arthur's court, floating up in the air—"

Beaufils got no further. The Père d'Arbé let out a

shriek and said, "The cups of wrath, filled with the last seven plagues! They've begun! And at King Arthur's court, too! So I was right! Arthur is the Beast from the Sea! It's Arthur!"

"Before you go any further," Gawain said, interrupting the hermit, "you ought to know that I am Arthur's nephew."

"Then you are the Second Beast!" the man said. "Begone! I am one of the Two Faithful Witnesses, and you cannot hurt me!"

The Père d'Arbé backed up against his hut, his limbs shaking. Gawain looked at him, the anger in his face slowly fading to pity, then jerked his head back to the forest. "Come on, let's go," he said. When the three friends were back among the trees, Gawain stopped and looked back at Beaufils. "I tried to warn you, lad."

"What was wrong with him?" Beaufils asked.

"Nothing we can help him with," Gawain replied. "I've met some of these birds before. There's a rule to follow here: If you ever hear anyone say the word *millennium*, don't ask them to explain what they mean." He sighed and added, "I'm starting to get tired of the Sacred Forest: isolated little huts, isolated holy men, and narrow little paths."

"What would happen if we left the path?" Beaufils mused aloud.

Gawain, who was leading again, stopped and looked over his shoulder at Beaufils. "I'd almost be willing to try it," he said.

"Why don't we?" asked Ellyn.

"Look how thick the shrubbery beside the path is," Gawain said. "If the whole forest is like this, we'll never get through."

"All right," Beaufils said. "It was just a thought. Let's stay on the path and ride on to the next hermit."

Gawain looked at him in silence, then began to laugh. "Touché, Le Beau. Off the path we go. You lead the way again, but don't go through too many tight squeezes. Remember that my horse is bigger than your mule."

Beaufils dismounted, took Clover's head, then plunged at once into the thickest part of the underbrush. For several minutes, he bent back twigs and pushed aside leafy fronds, unable to see more than a few feet ahead. Behind him he heard Ellyn and Gawain crashing in his steps. Suddenly he was out of the thickets in an open, sun-dappled forest. Tall pines stood around, but all at least twenty feet apart. The delicious smell of the trees filled his senses, and a springy bed of pine needles softened his footsteps. It was as if he had stepped out of a world of noise and into one of silence. Even the sound of Ellyn and Gawain thrashing through brush behind him seemed far away.

Then even their noise stopped. There was silence for a moment, broken at last by Gawain's reverent whisper. "Glory."

Beaufils grinned and clambered up onto Clover. "Let's go this way," he said.

After half an hour of blissfully peaceful riding, they came to the edge of the forest and to their last hermit. Because the forest was so open in this area, they saw the hermit's cottage well before they came to it—a simple, homely hut where a man in a brown robe was feeding a few goats in the front yard. Gawain halted his horse.

"Do we want to visit another one of these fellows?" he asked.

Ellyn hesitated. "I have to admit," she said, "I feel as if I've had all the holiness I can manage for a day. Do you think this one's like the others?"

Beaufils watched the man feed the goats for a moment, then said, "This one's already different from the others; he's taking care of someone else." Beaufils smiled and said, "Let's go look at the goats."

As they approached, Beaufils saw that this man was quite old. He didn't have much hair, but what he had was pure white, and the lines on his face seemed very deep, as if they had been carved in stone. But when the three riders approached, the hermit smiled genially. "Good evening," he said. "You must be Sir Gawain and

Lady Ellyn. And you"—he looked more closely at Beaufils—"must be the Fair Unknown."

"How did you know?" Beaufils asked, returning the hermit's smile.

"A friend told me to look for you," the hermit said. "I am Basil, the Hermit of the Forest's Edge."

"Not *Brother* Basil or *Father* Basil?" Beaufils asked.

"Not unless it really matters to you," the hermit replied. "I spend most of my time with the goats, and they don't care much about titles. Would you like some bread and milk?"

The travelers agreed, and dismounted. They cared for their mounts while Basil prepared a simple meal of brown bread, strawberries, and goat's milk to eat around an open fire in the yard. It seemed like a feast to Beaufils, and he ate with simple pleasure and gratitude, though he noticed that Gawain and Ellyn didn't seem thirsty. Basil said little at first, concerning himself only with his guests' needs, but after they had eaten, he asked, "And where have you been traveling today? In the Sacred Forest?"

"Is it only one day?" Gawain asked. "It seems much longer."

"How many hermits live in that forest anyway?" Ellyn asked.

"Heaven only knows," Basil replied. "They go on for

as long as the path continues. Did you enjoy meeting my fellow hermits?"

Gawain snorted, Ellyn rolled her eyes, and Beaufils replied, "They haven't been very helpful. Are you really a hermit too? You don't seem much like them."

"Yes, I'm really a hermit, too," Basil replied. "There's more goat's milk if anyone wants it."

Gawain and Ellyn quickly covered the tops of their cups, but Beaufils said thank you and took some more. "Then if we had just stayed on the path," he said, "we would have come to you eventually, right?"

"No," Basil replied. "There is one way in which I'm different from the others. To find me, you have to leave the path."

"Then I wish we'd just gone around the forest and skipped the path entirely," muttered Gawain.

"There's no way around it either," the hermit said.

"Sir," Gawain said suddenly, "may I ask a question?"

"You may ask anything, Sir Gawain."

"You said that a friend told you we would be coming this way. Who was this friend, and how did he know?"

"Was it a vision?" asked Ellyn.

"Oh, no," Basil replied, chuckling to himself. "I don't see visions myself. You'll have to leave that to some of my fellow hermits. Did you meet Brother Denys? He could see a vision for you."

"We met him," Gawain replied.

"Did you cry for him? I hope so." Beaufils shook his head, and Basil sighed. "Poor Denys. He feels awful when his visitors don't cry. No, my friend is as real as you are, but I couldn't say how he knew you'd be along. I'm only a simple man; I don't understand how Scotus knows what he knows. But I've learned to trust him."

"Scotus?" Gawain repeated.

"That's the enchanter who cursed my father," Ellyn said indignantly.

Basil nodded. "Yes, Lady Ellyn," Basil said. "I don't understand that either, but I was glad to hear that your father is better now." He glanced up at the darkening sky and said, "Forgive me for leaving you, but it is time for evening prayers. Excuse me."

While the hermit said his prayers, the three friends decided that they would stay the night with Basil— "Even if it means we have to drink more goat's milk tomorrow," Gawain said—and then leave the forest and head north again. By the time Basil returned, Ellyn had already rolled up in her blankets and gone to sleep. Gawain was getting his bed ready, but when Basil appeared, the knight addressed him.

"Excuse me, sir," he said, "I forgot to ask earlier. We're looking for something called the Holy Grail. I don't suppose you've heard of it, have you?"

"Yes, Sir Gawain. I know the Grail," Basil said.

"Oh," Gawain said, surprised. "That's helpful. Can you tell us where to find it?"

"Oh, dear me, Sir Gawain, you will never find the Grail," Basil said.

"What?"

"Didn't you know? The Grail is someone else's quest. The best you can do this time is to help others along, the way you've been helping Le Beau Desconus and Lady Ellyn."

Gawain took a moment to digest this, but he didn't seem to be disappointed. "Very well," he said at last, "and in which direction shall I help them tomorrow?"

"Oh, they don't need you now," Basil said. "Good night, Sir Gawain."

Basil went inside his hermitage, leaving Gawain standing uncertainly by the fire. At last he said, "I guess I can ask him in the morning what that means. You going to bed, Le Beau?"

"In a while," Beaufils said. Though his muscles were weary, he was oddly wakeful. Gawain went to his blankets and almost at once was breathing the deep, calm breaths of sleep.

"Gawain is a good man," said a voice at Beaufils's elbow. "I'm glad you've had a chance to travel with him."

Beaufils smiled, recognizing Scotus's voice. "Yes," he said.

"How have you found your journeying?" Scotus asked.

"I enjoy meeting new people," Beaufils replied simply. "Even people who don't seem to enjoy meeting me."

"That's a very good way to approach a quest."

"Am I on a quest?" Beaufils asked.

"Aren't you?"

"I suppose I am. This thing about the Grail. But I didn't say I would come because I wanted to find the Grail; I just thought it would be nice to ride with Galahad some more. Then Galahad went off, so I came with Gawain." Beaufils frowned, thinking, then said, "The Grail isn't really my quest, I think."

"Then do you have another quest?"

Beaufils thought about this. "Well, there's the thing about looking for my father, as my mother said to do. But if that's what I'm doing, then should I be out here hunting the Grail with Gawain?"

"Your father's as likely to be here as anywhere else, isn't he?" asked Scotus.

"I suppose," Beaufils said, but he was still troubled.

"Don't worry, son," Scotus said. "I've come to help. You've done all you can for Gawain, getting him through the forest, and now he has to go off alone. You're to go with Ellyn now for a while." Then Scotus was gone.

VII

THE LABORIOUS SAINT

Gawain protested vehemently the next morning when Basil told him he had to go on alone. Arguing that he was responsible for Lady Ellyn's safety and that he couldn't leave her in the care of an untried youth like Beaufils, Gawain grew so mulish that Basil had to speak to him very sternly.

"Sir Gawain," he said. "You still seem to feel that this is *your* quest, and that you shall have the ordering of it, but you are very much mistaken. I'm thinking about Lady Ellyn's quest. I know that you've sworn to protect fair womanhood, but protection is exactly what Lady Ellyn does not need. Le Beau Desconus is the only companion she requires."

"But what if—?" Gawain said.

"You can trust her to the Fair Unknown," Basil said with finality.

At last, obeying with ill grace but submitting nonetheless, Gawain mounted his great black horse and rode off alone. Beaufils watched until he was out of sight, then turned to Ellyn. "So which way do you want to go?"

"Me?"

"You know as well as I do," Beaufils said.

Ellyn smiled, closed her eyes, whirled around twice, and then pointed. "That way," she said. And they set off to the southeast.

It was a pleasant journey, the two of them riding side by side, talking about everything that came to mind and being comfortably silent when nothing did. They stopped to admire flowers and watch deer and cool their feet in streams. Often they dismounted and walked, saying they were resting the animals but knowing it was really just for the fun of walking. They were on foot, in fact, when they came upon the knight.

They had just gone up a hill and were starting down the other side when there he was, fully armored, in the middle of a field. He was on his knees, hands clasped and head bowed. They stopped in their tracks, staring, and then Beaufils recognized the knight's armor. "Sir Bors!" he exclaimed joyfully.

The knight raised his head, lifted his visor, then said,

"Beaufils? And a lady?" Then his eyes lit up. "And a horse!"

"What happened to Sir Lionel?" Beaufils asked. "And where's your horse?"

"Lionel and I separated a few days ago. We've joined a quest, you see, and we agreed that we could cover more ground separately."

"You're on a quest?" Beaufils asked, mildly interested. "It seems as if everyone's looking for something or other."

"This isn't just any quest, lad," Sir Bors said, lifting his chin. "It is a high and holy quest of great spiritual import. Lionel and I met some of Arthur's knights two days ago, and they told us about a miraculous vision that appeared in Arthur's court. Everyone's off seeking it."

"Oh," Beaufils said, nodding. "You're after the Grail."

"Er, yes," Sir Bors replied. "How did *you* know?"

"I was at the court when it appeared," Beaufils explained. "It was very pretty."

"Then you must have been sent to me as a guide!" Sir Bors exclaimed.

"Happy to help any way I can," Beaufils murmured.

"And this horse, too!" Sir Bors said excitedly. "You may not believe this, but I was just praying for God to send me a horse when you rode up! Isn't that amazing?"

"Except that this is *my* horse," Ellyn pointed out.

"Sir Bors, this is Lady Ellyn of Carlisle," Beaufils said. "And her horse."

"*Your* horse, my lady?" Sir Bors said.

"That's right."

"You wouldn't want to give him up?"

"No."

"Sell him?"

"No."

"Lend him?"

"No."

Sir Bors frowned with puzzlement. "I don't understand. I prayed and everything."

Ellyn's face was growing stormy, and Beaufils thought it time to intervene. "Perhaps the two of you could share."

"I wouldn't mind that," Ellyn said slowly. "But Sir Bors hasn't asked."

"Oh," Sir Bors said. "Um . . . could we share your horse for a bit?"

"Of course," Ellyn said. Beaufils wondered why her eyes had begun to twinkle. "You climb on first, and then I'll get up behind you."

Sir Bors thanked her graciously, then put his foot in the horse's stirrup and swung his leg over. "Ouch!" he said.

"Uncomfortable?" asked Ellyn, suppressing a smile.

"This saddle! It's poking me right in the . . . I mean . . ."

"It's a sidesaddle, you see," Ellyn explained. "Was that not what you prayed for?"

"I can't ride like this! This pommel goes right up . . . I should say . . . Why, every time the horse jumped it would . . . um . . . hurt."

"Don't you have armor on?" Ellyn asked sweetly.

"Not down there!"

"I wonder why not," she mused.

Sir Bors swung his leg back over and dismounted. "You can have your horse back."

"Would you like to ride Clover?" Beaufils asked. "I don't mind walking."

Sir Bors looked at the mule distastefully, then said, "Thank you, Beaufils, but no. No, I don't think so."

"Well, at any rate, we can travel together," Beaufils said. "We don't mind traveling slow." This being agreed to, they started off again, all three walking. Beaufils glanced at Sir Bors and said, "But you never said what happened to *your* horse."

Sir Bors scowled. "It was stolen from me!" he said fiercely. "Just after Lionel and I parted, three knights came on me and attacked. I was driven from the saddle and almost killed!"

"You seem all right. I suppose the knights spared your life?" Ellyn asked.

"Not by choice!" Sir Bors exclaimed. "I'm sure they meant to finish me off, but I was rescued by a strange knight with silver armor who galloped up on a white horse. I promise you, I've never seen his like. Sword here, shield there, and in a trice all three knights were on the run. Then the silver knight rode away. The thing is, though, the three knights took my horse with them."

"White horse and silver armor?" Beaufils asked. "Did his shield have a red cross on it?"

"Yes, it did!"

"Oh, that was Galahad," Beaufils said. "Good for him."

"Who's Galahad?" Sir Bors asked. "I've never heard the name."

"He's Sir Lancelot's son," Beaufils explained.

"What?"

"Didn't the knights who told you about the Grail tell you about Galahad? It seems that Sir Lancelot fathered Galahad many years ago and never knew he had a son. The same as my father must have done."

Sir Bors blinked, then, in an apologetic voice, said, "I had forgotten your quest, Beaufils. Did you ever find your father?"

Beaufils sighed. "No, not yet. Sir Lionel was right: it seems it could have been nearly anyone."

Sir Bors lapsed into silence, and they trudged on together without speaking. Beaufils didn't mind this. Birds were singing, and he saw several flowers that he'd never seen before. Sometimes, he reflected, it was nice to talk, but other times it was nice to let the world talk back.

The world's speech was brief, however. A few minutes later, Sir Bors emitted a deep sigh, then groaned, "I cannot keep it within!"

"Are you feeling queasy, Sir Bors?" Beaufils asked, concerned. "Something you ate?"

"I should have told you when I first met you, but I was afraid. I hoped another knight would prove to be the one. But now I must speak. Beaufils, I . . . I may be your father myself."

Beaufils smiled. "Wouldn't that be nice?"

Sir Bors didn't seem to hear; he was intent on his next words. "It was nearly eighteen years ago. My father wanted me to be a knight, like my brother Lionel, but I was inclined toward the priesthood. My father thought that a visit to court would cure me of my religious ideas, so he sent me to Camelot. And, in truth, he was right. As soon as I arrived there, I was carried away by worldly pleasures!"

Not sure what was expected of him, Beaufils nodded and said, "Yes, I enjoyed my visit to Camelot, too."

"I don't see anything so bad about a holiday at court," Ellyn remarked. "I'd love one myself."

"You don't understand," Sir Bors said. "There was this servant girl . . ."

"Ah, I see," Ellyn said. "What happened to the girl?"

Bors looked up, surprise on his face. "I left the court shortly after that, but a year or so later I heard that she married one of the smithies and moved away. So you see, Beaufils! I may well be your father!"

Ellyn snorted and commented, "I don't know what Beau was expecting from his long-lost father, but I doubt it was such a gloomy reception as this. You look more like you've just lost a son than found one."

Sir Bors looked struck by this. "Forgive me, Beaufils. I wasn't thinking of you."

"No, you weren't," Ellyn said. "You might try it now."

Sir Bors looked solemnly at Beaufils. "Can you forgive me, lad?"

Beaufils smiled. "I wish I could, if it would make you happy, but I'm afraid I've nothing to forgive."

"Eh?" asked Sir Bors, confused.

Beaufils explained. "The girl you remember couldn't be my mother. You said that she got married and moved away a year or so after the two of you had your meeting, didn't you? Well, I don't know how long a woman will carry a child before—"

"Nine months," Ellyn said.

"That long? That must be a bother. But you see what I'm getting at, don't you? My mother left Camelot before I was born, so she couldn't have hung about for a year or so. I'm afraid you aren't my father after all."

"Oh, I see," Sir Bors said. Then his brows drew together. "You mean I made my confession to you for nothing?"

"You can't say that," replied Ellyn. "Maybe it did *you* some good."

"At any rate, it helped to pass the time," Beaufils added cheerfully. "What shall we talk about now?"

For the next hour or so, Beaufils and Ellyn had to conduct whatever conversation there was to have. Sir Bors remained gloomily silent. Eventually, though, he discovered another fruitful subject—the discomfort of walking in armor, which led, by natural progression, to the subject of what he'd like to do to the knights who had taken his horse. This didn't contribute much to the conversation, as there was little that Beaufils and Ellyn could add, but Sir Bors didn't need their help to expound on the subject of his own aches and blisters and plans for revenge.

Beaufils tried to be understanding, but since Sir Bors had refused his offer to ride Clover, it was hard to sympathize. So it was with relief that he saw someone else approaching them over the heath. It was a woman, and she was leading a very large and powerful-looking horse.

"Good morrow, fair lady," called out Sir Bors, sweeping a bow to her.

"Good morrow, Sir Knight," the lady replied. She

137

had long, flowing hair that hung down around her shiny red dress. "But what is this? A handsome knight on foot? How can this be?"

Sir Bors bowed again. "I am indeed grieved to appear so before so beautiful a lady. Indeed, it was not my fault! Three scurrilous knights set upon me without warning and stole my mount from me."

"Three knights against one!" the woman exclaimed with horror. "Why, you must be a knight of great valor to have escaped with your life!"

Sir Bors hesitated, then shook his head. "I am afraid I can claim no valor, my lady. I was rescued by another knight."

The woman let a trill of laughter escape. "Why, you are a conscientious knight!"

"Thank you, my lady. I try," Sir Bors said, bowing again.

Beaufils had moved close to Ellyn during this exchange, and now he whispered to her. "Is this lady beautiful?"

Ellyn looked surprised. "Can't you tell?"

Beaufils shook his head. "No. I enjoy looking at everyone. But other people seem to prefer certain features over others."

Ellyn smiled at Beaufils with sudden warmth. "Yes," she said. "This woman is what most men would consider beautiful. *Very* beautiful."

"Men? But not women?"

Ellyn lowered her voice. "She's all right, I suppose. But any woman would think she's a silly goose to wear that silk dress out for a stroll in the fields."

The beautiful goose clapped her hands together suddenly. "Why, Sir Knight! How silly I am!"

"There, you see?" Ellyn whispered.

"You say that you were set upon by three knights? And they stole your horse? But not five minutes ago three knights passed along this very road, and they were leading another horse!"

"They were here!" Sir Bors exclaimed excitedly. "My lady! I must ask your favor. Will you permit me to borrow your horse?"

"Oh, I could never do that," the lady said. "Ginger here has been my pet since he was a colt! No one else has ever ridden him, and I love him as I would a child."

"I would take the very best care of your horse, but you must see, my lady, that I have lost honor by my earlier defeat, and here is a chance for me to reclaim it!"

Beaufils frowned. "But if they knocked you off your horse last time—" he began.

"Last time they took me by surprise!" Sir Bors replied promptly. "This time I shall take *them* by surprise. Please, my lady, you must see how important it is!"

The lady hesitated. "I do, Sir Knight, and I would do

anything in my power to help you recover your honor, but I love Ginger so! If I let you borrow him, will I ever see him again?"

"But of course, my lady! I shall return him to you at once after my victory. Just tell me where to take him."

"I am the Lady Orgille, and my home is Orgille Hall, three miles to the east. Oh, what shall I do?" She took a deep breath that made her chest bob up and down. Then she handed the reins to Sir Bors. "Here, Sir Knight. Do not fail me. Bring my beloved pet back as soon as you are able."

"I swear it!" Sir Bors shouted, leaping into the saddle. He looked briefly at Ellyn and Beaufils and said, "You stay here! I want to take them by surprise, and too many riders might alert them of my approach!" Then he was off, thundering down the path in a manner likely to alert everyone for miles around.

Lady Orgille smiled very faintly, then began to walk back the way she had come. Beaufils said, "Er, Lady Orgille? Do you need any help getting home?" But she either didn't hear or didn't care to answer, because she continued striding away.

"There's something not right here," Ellyn said. "I don't trust that Orgille."

"Why not?" inquired Beaufils.

"Well, there's the silk dress. No lady would wear that

for a solitary ride out in the fields. You'd only wear something like that if you were expecting someone and wanted to make an impression. A man. And that was no lady's horse either. A great big animal like that?"

Beaufils, of course, knew nothing of dresses and horses, but he had no trouble accepting Ellyn's doubts as valid. "Ellyn," he said. "That sidesaddle of yours. Do all ladies use that sort of saddle?"

Ellyn's eyes widened. "You're right, Beau! Lady Orgille said that horse was her own and no one else had ever ridden it, but it had a man's saddle!"

"As if she were planning to lend it to a man," Beaufils said.

Ellyn frowned for a moment, then waved her hands at Beaufils. "Let me think."

Beaufils cleared his throat. "Could you think while riding? I have a feeling that Sir Bors might be in trouble up ahead."

Ellyn nodded. "That's what I was thinking," she said.

Fifteen minutes later, they found that they'd been right. Riding through a craggy area, where the path led through several tall boulders, they came upon Sir Bors, unhurt but trudging dejectedly back down the path toward them. Lady Orgille's horse was gone.

"Oh, dear," Ellyn said.

"Are you hurt?" asked Beaufils.

"Only my honor," replied Sir Bors, his voice flat. "I have lost my own horse, and now I have lost the Lady Orgille's." A sudden hope sprang into his eyes. "Lady Ellyn, could I borrow your horse? I'd take off the saddle and ride bareback, but I must—"

"You must have been hit in the head," she said. "Why would I trust you with my horse, with your history?"

Sir Bors drooped, as much as someone in armor can droop, then nodded. "You're right. I can't be trusted at all, can I?"

"Listen to us, Sir Bors," Ellyn said. "We were thinking about this Lady Orgille. We think she was waiting for you."

Sir Bors shook his head slowly and resumed plodding down the path.

"Didn't you hear me?" Ellyn said. "She *meant* for you to take that horse. Didn't you think it strange that it was saddled with a—?"

"It makes no difference," Sir Bors said gloomily. "Though she were a fiend from hell, I should still have to return to her and humble myself before her. I took her horse, promising to return it, and now I've lost it. I've done her a great wrong."

Beaufils and Ellyn looked at each other. "I guess so," Ellyn said with a resigned shrug as they trailed behind the trudging knight. "You have to admit that Sir Bors always does what he thinks is right."

Beaufils nodded, but uncertainly. "Yes," he said. "But is doing right supposed to make you so unhappy?"

"No!" moaned Lady Orgille. "No! Oh, poor Ginger! My beloved pet, my dear, my darling who ate sugar from my hand when I was a mere child!"

They were in a large room at Orgille Hall, to which they had been conducted by a servant. Lady Orgille had joined them there, wearing a different gown—of the same shiny material but fitting her body even more snugly. Sir Bors, with great resolution, had plunged at once into his confession, which led Lady Orgille to place her hand on her chest and wail and moan and look like she was sick. Ellyn, standing beside Beaufils, looked grim.

"My lady," Sir Bors said, kneeling. "I shall do all in my power to restore your beast to you."

"On foot?" demanded Lady Orgille between sobs. "What can you do?"

"I can do little, I know. But I vow that all that I can do—"

"And meanwhile the White Knight will steal my lands!" moaned the lady.

"Eh? What White Knight?" asked Sir Bors.

Lady Orgille took several deep breaths, as if to calm herself. Beaufils wasn't sure that her dress would hold, but it must have been well made, because no matter how much air she took in, none of the seams popped. At last she seemed able to speak. "My lands are under siege," she said. "Or they will be soon. A strange knight, clad entirely in white armor, has come to this land and has declared that he will soon be the lord of my lands. And I have no knights to defend me."

Sir Bors took Lady Orgille's hand. "Command me, my lady. What do you wish me to do?"

For a moment, Beaufils caught an odd look in Lady Orgille's eyes, a flicker of satisfaction. Then she took another of her deep breaths and sighed. "I hardly know, Sir Knight. But if you would be willing to fight for me—oh, perhaps then I might be saved."

"You have only to summon me, my lady. I am Sir Bors, of the Fellowship of the Round Table, and I will lay my life and my honor at your feet."

"A knight of Camelot!" exclaimed Lady Orgille with a gasp. "Oh, I shall be saved after all!" Another deep breath. Then, with her right hand, she reached down the front of her gown and pulled out a white square of cloth. "Sir Bors, do you see this embroidered handkerchief?"

"Yes, my lady."

"When I need you, I shall send this token. Will you vow to come to me at once when you see this?"

"I vow it with all my heart, my lady!"

"No matter what else you may be doing?"

"Indeed, I promise!"

Lady Orgille sighed, then smiled. "Then I can be at peace again." She clapped her hands, and a servant appeared. "Gorin!" she said. "Take Sir Bors to the stables! Give him the finest horse there! He will be our champion!"

"My lady!" stammered Sir Bors, overwhelmed at the gift of the horse.

"We cannot leave our savior and champion afoot, can we? I thank you, Sir Bors. Keep your vow to help me, and I . . . I will look forward to your return." Lady Orgille blushed and lowered her eyes.

"Now," Beaufils whispered to Ellyn. "Deep breath coming."

Lady Orgille took a deep breath. Ellyn looked as if she had just tasted something nasty, but she didn't speak as she and the two men followed the servant to the stables, chose a horse for Sir Bors, and then rode away together.

VIII

THE TESTING OF SIR BORS

"Can't you see that she was using you?" Ellyn snapped at Sir Bors. "The whole thing was a plot to get you on her side against this White Knight!"

"Then why didn't she say so at once? She didn't have to go through all this handkerchief business; I would have helped her anyway. Any of Arthur's knights would," replied Sir Bors mulishly.

"Maybe, but without your vow you might have asked a few questions first. As it is, she's got you under oath, and she won't let that advantage go to waste. You'll see that hanky again, and soon."

Sir Bors scowled but did not reply, and the three continued down the path toward the rocks where Sir Bors had lost Lady Orgille's horse. There was a sharp bend ahead, where the road curved around a massive dome of rock, and as they came to this curve they heard a burst of raucous laughter from around the corner. Sir Bors smiled and loosened his sword in its sheath. "Perhaps I will have another chance at these knights," he said. He seemed pleased by the prospect. In light of the way the first two meetings had turned out, Beaufils wasn't sure why.

Rounding the bend, the three beheld a piteous sight. In an open area among the boulders stood three knights, and tethered nearby were five horses. One of the horses was Sir Bors's old horse, Beaufils noticed, but Lady Orgille's beloved Ginger was not there. The fifth horse, he decided, must belong to the fourth man in the clearing, who was stretched out face-down on the path, his hands and feet tied and staked to the ground. Below the waist he wore armor, but he was naked from the chest up, and his back was covered with blood. The three knights who stood around him had removed their helms and iron gauntlets and each held in his bare hand a long branch covered with thorns. Clearly, they had been beating the man on the ground with these thorny switches.

"You three are despicable," Sir Bors said, drawing his sword and riding into the middle of the clearing. "You don't deserve the name of knight. Release that man and draw your swords."

A faint drumming sound from behind came to

Beaufils's ears. Someone was riding toward them on the path—one horse. At that moment, the bound and bleeding man lifted his head, with effort, and looked up at Sir Bors. "Bors?" he groaned.

"Lionel!" gasped Sir Bors. "By all that's holy, you men shall pay for this!" The three knights glanced at each other nervously and took a step back, reaching for their weapons. Sir Bors already had his blade ready and was about to charge into the three, but suddenly a liveried servant on horseback pounded into the clearing.

"Sir Bors!" the servant shouted.

"I'll be with you in a moment," Sir Bors said calmly, never taking his eyes from the three knights.

"You must come with me at once!" the servant said.

"I said you'll have to wait."

The servant replied in a ringing voice, "This handkerchief says otherwise!"

Sir Bors froze, then glanced quickly over his shoulder at the little square of cloth that the servant was waving. "Oh, blast," he said.

Beaufils's heart sank as he saw what was about to happen. Sir Bors, with his rigid sense of honor, would not break his solemn promise to Lady Orgille.

"Bors?" gasped Sir Lionel.

Sir Bors's face was blank, but his eyes were filled with anguish. "Lionel, I . . ."

"Help me," Sir Lionel said.

"The thing is . . . there's this lady . . ."

"Bors!"

Sir Bors set his jaw. "I'll be back for you, Lionel." Then he whirled his horse and galloped away with the servant.

"Bors!" shouted Sir Lionel furiously. The three knights grinned and looked at Beaufils and Ellyn.

"Now that young lady is quite an eyeful," said one of them, stepping forward.

"Beaufils?" Ellyn said.

Beaufils saw at once that they couldn't run. The knights' great horses would catch them easily. Beaufils grasped his cudgel and slipped from Clover's back. He stepped between Ellyn and the knights, then walked toward them.

The nearest knight, the one who had spoken first, gave a grunt of laughter. "The boy's going to fight three of us with a stick?"

"I don't want to fight," Beaufils replied, stepping still closer.

"I'll wager you don't," chortled one of the other knights. "But it makes no—"

Beaufils was now only a few feet away from the nearest knight, who reached for the sword at his side. Beaufils immediately bashed the knight's bare hand with his cudgel. "Ouch!" the knight shouted, snatching his hand away from his sword. The next knight reached for his sword, and Beaufils smashed his hand in the same way. The second knight screamed and put his fingers in his mouth while Beaufils ducked under a ponderous punch from the first knight and rapped the third knight's fingers with his cudgel, as he had the first two.

"Now you should let this man go," Beaufils said, stepping away from the pack.

This time the knights all went for their swords at the same time. Beaufils was able to smash the first one's hand again, but the other two got their swords free and began swinging at him. Beaufils ducked under one blade and stepped out of reach of the second. It was harder to hit the knights' hands now that they were waving swords, but he managed to bash one knight's free hand, making him howl with pain. The first knight, who still hadn't drawn his sword, came within range, and though he was still unarmed Beaufils no longer had leisure to pick his targets or to aim at hands. With all his strength, he clubbed the knight in the back of the head. The man made a soft sound—something like "blk"— then fell on his face in the dust, tripping one of his companions, who was rushing at Beaufils. To evade another swing from the third knight, Beaufils had to throw himself sharply to one side. A stone rolled under his foot, and he sprawled in the dirt behind Clover and Ellyn's horse. The third knight charged toward him, roaring with glee, then stopped and stood triumphantly over

Beaufils's prone form. He raised his sword above his head and then, to Beaufils's considerable surprise, appeared to jump a foot in the air and fling himself against a rock, where he dropped his blade and crumpled in a ball on the ground, moaning.

Beaufils didn't understand this last bit, but he didn't object. Scrambling to his feet, he turned to face the last knight again, only to see him kneeling at the feet of Sir Lionel, who held a sword to his throat. Ellyn, still holding the knife with which she had cut Sir Lionel's bonds, stood just behind them.

"Mercy?" whispered the kneeling knight.

"You're asking mercy from the knight you just flogged with wild rose branches?" Sir Lionel replied.

"It was just a bit of fun, sir," the knight said helplessly. "Meaning no harm."

"You know what I think would be fun?" Sir Lionel answered.

"Letting me go?" the knight suggested plaintively.

Sir Lionel drew back his sword, then brought the haft down on the knight's head with a dull thump. The knight pitched forward on his face, and Sir Lionel said, "Meaning no harm, of course." He turned toward Beaufils and managed a smile. "Beaufils," he said, "I didn't know you at first, but I recognized your knack with that club. Thank you." Then he turned to Ellyn. "And thank *you*, my lady."

All seemed to be well, which permitted Beaufils to satisfy his curiosity on another matter. "Say," he said. "What happened to the fellow who was about to kill me? He just seemed to fly against that rock all at once."

A dimple appeared on Ellyn's cheek. "Besides being a recreant knight, he wasn't very clever. He didn't even know not to stand behind an agitated mule."

Beaufils's eyes widened with sudden sympathy. "Clover kicked him all that way? I hope he isn't too badly hurt." He stepped over beside the fallen knight, taking care to toss the knight's sword out of reach, then knelt beside him. "Where did Clover kick you, sir?" he asked.

The knight only groaned and writhed. Ellyn stepped up beside Beaufils and examined the knight dispassionately. "Must have gotten him somewhere he didn't have armor," she said. "He looks as though he'll survive, though."

Seeing nothing else to do, Beaufils stood and turned back to the others. "Well, what do we do now?"

"First of all, Beaufils," Sir Lionel said, "will you introduce me to your enchanting friend?"

"Oh, I'm sorry. Sir Lionel, this is Lady Ellyn of Carlisle. Ellyn, this is Sir Bors's brother, Sir Lionel."

"His brother?" Ellyn exclaimed. "He ran off and left his own brother?"

"Oh, did you notice that too?" said Sir Lionel bitterly.

"It had to do with that hanky," Beaufils explained to

Sir Lionel. "You see, he had made a vow to drop every-thing and go help this lady whenever she sent him that token. He must have thought he had to honor his promise."

From their expressions, Beaufils could see that nei-ther Sir Lionel nor Ellyn thought much of Sir Bors's priorities. Beaufils sympathized with them. Why was it so hard to admire Sir Bors's commitment to his oath?

For the next few minutes they discussed what to do with the three incapacitated knights. At last they decided to break their swords, which Sir Lionel said was a dis-grace to a knight, then take away their armor and horses, thus stripping them of all signs of knighthood. As Beaufils and Ellyn and Sir Lionel rode off, leading the other four horses, Beaufils said, "Shall we go see if Sir Bors needs help?"

Sir Lionel laughed harshly. "And why should I care?" he asked.

"I don't know," Beaufils said. "But I do. Will you come with me?"

Sir Lionel shook his head. "Somehow," he said bleakly, "I just can't see going to help Bors right now." With that, he gave his own horse a kick and trotted away without a backward glance.

Beaufils glanced inquiringly at Ellyn.

"Let's see if he needs us," she said. "He's an ass, but I don't wish him harm."

When they arrived at Orgille Hall, the gates were open and the courtyard empty. If it weren't for the distant sound of shouting from the far side of the castle, Beaufils would have thought it was entirely deserted. "What's going on?" he wondered aloud.

"Let's take all these horses to the stable, then go see," Ellyn suggested.

They rode to the stable, where one elderly hostler limped out to them. "Brought them home, have you?" he wheezed, glancing at the horses behind them. Then he nodded at Sir Bors's old horse. "With a new one, I see. Where are Rufus, Caron, and Brock?"

Ellyn's jaw tightened. "You mean the three knights who ride these horses? Do they live here?"

"When they ain't running errands for My Lady," the old groom said, taking the reins of the knights' horses from Beaufils's hand. "Come on in, boys."

Beaufils stopped the hostler. "Just a moment, old man," he said. "Can you tell us where everyone is?"

The old man shrugged. "Likely they're all up on the back wall watching the fight."

"What fight?" Ellyn demanded.

"My Lady's managed to finagle another knight into fighting Sir Erskine," the groom replied. "Third one this month. Don't know why anyone's bothering to watch."

"Who's Sir Erskine?" Beaufils and Ellyn inquired together.

"He's the brother of the old lord, the one who died sudden-like a week or two after he took My Lady in as his mistress. By rights, Erskine's the owner of the castle, but My Lady's held him off so far."

"I suppose Sir Erskine wears white armor," Ellyn said, nodding to herself.

"That's the fellow. Me, I don't care much either way. I take care of the horses and let the lords and ladies fight as much as suits them." With that, the man disappeared into the stable, leading the knights' three horses.

"What do we do?" Ellyn asked.

"Let's go see if we can help Sir Bors."

"And maybe help Sir Erskine," added Ellyn.

"That too."

Beaufils wasn't sure what to do, but as they rode, leading Sir Bors's horse up to the field where two knights fought with swords, he decided that whatever else happened, Sir Bors needed to know the true state of affairs. So, at the edge of the field, he dismounted and began to call, "Sir Bors! Sir Bors!"

"He can't hear you out there, with all that banging," Ellyn said.

"And with his helm on, too," Beaufils said. "I'll have to get closer." For the second time that day, he drew his cudgel from his gear and strode toward a fight.

When he was about five yards from the combatants, he realized that Sir Bors and Sir Erskine were speaking to each other, in gasps. "I know," Sir Bors was saying. "But I took a vow."

Sir Erskine swung an overhand blow at Sir Bors, which was easily parried. "Must you keep a vow to a woman like that? She would keep no vow to you."

"It makes—" Sir Bors broke off to lash out at Sir Erskine. He missed and staggered briefly. "—no difference! If I break my vow it dishonors me, not her."

"Excuse me," Beaufils said.

"We're busy, boy," Sir Erskine said.

"Beaufils?" gasped Sir Bors.

"Yes. How are the two of you doing?"

"Go away," the two knights said in unison.

"Sir Erskine?" Beaufils continued. "How do you do? My name is Beaufils, or at least that's what I go by."

Sir Erskine rushed at Sir Bors, using his shield as a weapon, trying to drive his opponent to the ground by sheer weight. Bors managed to evade the brunt of the blow, but he staggered to one side and barely managed to block a thrust from Sir Erskine's sword.

"I said that my name is Beaufils," Beaufils continued.

Sir Erskine whirled about, his sword at the ready. "Charmed, I'm sure," he said, panting.

"I'm a friend of Sir Bors, but I'd like to help you too, if I can."

The two knights crossed swords, then ran together, just like two boars fighting over territory. Beaufils had to step quickly out of their way, but he didn't back off. When they separated, Sir Bors said, "I don't see how . . . you can help us both, lad . . . We're fighting."

"Yes, I noticed that. The thing is, you were tricked into fighting Sir Erskine here."

"Think I don't know that, lad?" Sir Bors said, swinging a heavy blow at Sir Erskine's legs that was parried only at the last second.

"How do you know?" Beaufils asked.

"When I got here . . . to the castle . . . I saw Lady Orgille's horse in the stable."

"Ginger?"

"Ay," Sir Bors said. "The one she lent—" He had to break off to meet another lunge of Sir Erskine's. They grappled, both of their swords useless at close range, then toppled over and began rolling on the ground. Beaufils skipped out of their way, then approached them from the other side.

"That makes sense," Beaufils said, nodding. "It turns out that those three knights who kept taking horses from you work for Lady Orgille."

From the pile of armored legs and arms came a response from Sir Bors. It was muffled, but it might have been, "Fascinating."

"So anyway," Beaufils said. "I was thinking that maybe you shouldn't be fighting Sir Erskine here."

Sir Erskine managed to draw his knee up between

himself and Sir Bors and thrust him away, breaking each man's grip on the other. Both knights immediately swung their swords at the other, but both missed. They scrambled to their feet.

"I swore an oath!" Sir Bors rapped out grimly. Sir Erskine attacked again, and again Sir Bors fought off the assault.

"Yes, I know," Beaufils said. "But look at it this way. You promised to fight the White Knight. Well, you've fought him now. You can stop anytime."

"You know very well that when I made my promise, I meant—"

"Look here, fellow," interrupted Sir Erskine. "Are you even paying attention to me? Who is this boy?"

"Didn't I introduce myself?" Beaufils said. "Yes, I'm sure I did. Twice, in fact. I said my name is Beaufils, and you said that you were charmed. It's very nice to meet you, too."

"Yes, yes," Sir Erskine said. He and Sir Bors were circling each other just out of sword's reach, so Beaufils began to trot next to Sir Erskine. "I remember now," the knight said. "It's just that this isn't the best time for me, you know?"

"I'd rather meet you now than wait until you've been killed," Beaufils said. "That wouldn't be very pleasant at all."

"Maybe I won't be killed," Sir Erskine said. "I hadn't planned on it."

"Neither had I," retorted Sir Bors at once.

"There, you see? It's a hopeless case," Beaufils said reasonably.

"I will not break my vow," Sir Bors repeated doggedly.

"But if you won't stop fighting, then the only way to keep your vow will be to kill Sir Erskine. Do you really want to do that?"

"No!" Sir Bors said. "But I have no choice."

"What a silly thing to say!" exclaimed Beaufils. "You could lay down your sword and say you're sorry and that you made a mistake."

"I most certainly cannot!" Sir Bors declared with revulsion.

"Why not? On the way here you told us all about your sins. Why is it easier to confess to us than to apologize to Sir Erskine?"

"I would lose my honor!"

"But you wouldn't lose it by killing a man for no good reason?"

"No!"

"This honor stuff is very confusing," Beaufils complained, still trotting around the outside of the circling knights. "And I'm not sure it's very helpful. Why is keeping your honor more important than Sir Erskine keeping his life?"

The knights probed each other with their swords, but their thrusts were weak. Beaufils continued. "I know, Sir Bors, that you always try to do what's right. It's one of the things I like about you. But you don't have a choice between right and wrong here. Either you break your promise or you kill an innocent man."

"I don't know why you're so sure Sir Bors here will win," Sir Erskine said suddenly. "I'm not so bad. I beat the last two knights that Orgille sent against me, didn't I?"

"Maybe that's the solution," Sir Bors said in a low voice. "Maybe I should be killed. Then Sir Erskine keeps his life and I keep my honor."

"That's a terrible idea!" Beaufils said. "You're daft."

"He is, isn't he?" Sir Erskine said, lowering his sword. "Look here, fellow. I respect the fact that you made a promise and want to keep it. But I don't want to fight you anymore."

Sir Bors lowered his sword. "Why not? Are you afraid?"

"It's just that my mother taught me to be kind to idiots," Sir Erskine retorted.

"You'll pay for that insult!"

Sir Erskine lifted his head high but kept his arms at his side. "Go ahead, then. Hit me. I won't stop you."

"You won't?" Sir Bors asked. He lowered his own sword. "I can't hit you while you're just standing like that!"

"Let me guess," Beaufils said. "You would lose your honor if you did?"

"That's right."

"I figured there'd be a rule about that," Beaufils said. "You know what I think? I think you have too many rules."

"So you think I should hit him?" Sir Bors demanded.

"No," Beaufils replied patiently. "I think you should go tell Lady Orgille that you've changed your mind and you're not going to keep your silly promise after all. Then I think you ought to ride away with Ellyn and me on your own horse, which we brought with us."

Sir Bors stood very still, his sword arm limp at his side. Then he took a deep breath and said, "All right, blast you both. All right."

Sir Bors was morose and silent again as they rode away from Orgille Hall, and Beaufils was beginning to wonder if there was some way that he and Ellyn could part from their moody friend. His fierce gloom cast a shadow over what would otherwise have been a splendid day for a ride, and squelched all conversation. Beaufils and Ellyn hadn't even felt able to tell him that his brother Lionel was all right, and Sir Bors hadn't asked.

Sir Bors was probably ruminating on his painful interview with Lady Orgille. As Beaufils had suggested, he had walked to the foot of the wall from which the lady and her court were watching the battle and called up that he was not going to kill Sir Erskine for her after all. Then Sir Bors had stood stoically beneath the wall while Lady Orgille had called him a villain and a coward and a great many other things, mostly involving words that Beaufils didn't know. Sir Bors had made no answer, but when at last the storm of abuse had ended, Lady Orgille having exhausted either her voice or her vocabulary, Sir Bors had simply bowed once more, mounted his horse, and ridden away. Now, an hour later, he still had not spoken.

Beaufils was starting to feel bored and had just about decided to begin talking normally to Ellyn again regardless of Sir Bors's scowls when they came to an austere cottage in the midst of a small, cleared area. Beaufils heard Ellyn sigh. "A hermit," she said softly.

From the hut came a thin man with a long neck. He was wearing the plain brown robe that seemed to be the standard uniform of holy men, although Beaufils noticed that this particular robe looked as if it was much more comfortable than others he had seen. Sir Bors brightened at the approach of the hermit. "A holy man!" he breathed thankfully.

The hermit looked aloofly at the three travelers. "Am

I to have no peace in which to meditate?" he asked querulously.

"Father," Sir Bors said, nearly throwing himself from his horse. "I need to confess."

"You sound like that Galahad fellow," the hermit complained. "Wouldn't even let me finish my supper, he was in such a blazing hurry to confess, just as if he'd committed every mortal sin in the book, which he hadn't. Then that other fellow, earlier today, nearly kicking the door in asking for food, though I'd like to know where he thought I'd get food. Some people think that all we holy men do with our lives is store up food to hand over to every jackanapes that wanders by. Why not? What else does a hermit have to do? Let me tell you, it takes nearly all my time just to keep up with my prayers. And the wood isn't chopped, and the roof needs work, too. Well? Are you going to confess or just grovel?"

Beaufils and Ellyn exchanged glances at this speech, but Sir Bors evidently saw nothing amiss and plunged at once into a full description of the recent events in his life, starting with his foolish vow to Lady Orgille, continuing through his leaving Lionel to his tormentors, and concluding with his breaking his promise and riding away. Listening to this account, Beaufils wasn't sure which of these events Sir Bors regarded as sins and which he did not. Maybe he was hoping the hermit would tell him. When he was done, the holy man gazed silently at Sir Bors, a speculative light in his eyes. "Please, Father," Sir Bors said, sinking to his knees, "give me my penance—anything!"

"You want penance?" the hermit grumbled. "How about going away and leaving me alone?"

Sir Bors hesitated. "That's not much, is it? Shouldn't you make me do more? After all, I left my own brother to die."

"Er, Sir Bors," Beaufils began, "about Sir Lionel—"

But Sir Bors pressed on. "I heard once about a knight who had to wear a hair shirt under his armor for years as a penance, just like a hermit. Or rather, I mean . . . *is* that a hair shirt you're wearing?"

"I can't wear hair shirts!" the hermit snapped. "I have sensitive skin! You want penance? Fine! Go cut some wood for me!"

Sir Bors bowed his head obediently. "Yes, Father. And will that be all?"

The hermit suddenly looked thoughtful. "Er, no, that's not all," he said slowly. "Dear me, no. You *have* been very bad, haven't you? I shall have to pray about this. Yes, I have it! Sir Bors, you must renounce your arms for the space of one, no, *two* years, and must assume the humiliation of being a servant! Right here, so that I—your Father Confessor—can keep an eye on your soul's health. You must cut wood and carry water and keep a garden and hunt wild game—all to humble your soul, that you might be spared from this most horrible sin."

Sir Bors looked up slowly at the hermit's face, his own expression a mixture of grief and doubt. "So to cleanse my soul I need to become your slave for two years?"

"It's not like that," the hermit said hastily. "It will be a trial to me, as well. I daresay you'll disturb my life of meditation awfully with all that work."

Gravel crunched from the far side of the little clearing, and Beaufils looked up to see the swiftly striding figure of Sir Lionel himself. He crossed the yard in a flash, then drew back his ironclad foot and kicked Sir Bors with great force in the part of his hindquarters without armor, launching him forward into the hermit's legs.

"Ouch!" shouted Sir Bors, whirling around. "Who the devil . . . Lionel?"

"Who'd you think, you stupid sod!"

"I thought you were dead!"

"If I'm not, it's no thanks to you," Sir Lionel retorted wrathfully. "Here, let's see if I feel like a ghost, shall we?" He kicked at his brother again, but Sir Bors scrambled backward on his hands and feet, and only received a glancing blow.

"Lionel, listen to me!"

"Go ahead," Sir Lionel said, striding forward. "I'll kick you a bit while I listen, shall I?" He got another solid kick in, but this time his armored foot only clanked harmlessly against the iron cuisse on his brother's left thigh.

"I was wrong!" Sir Bors shouted. He was still on his back, but he had raised himself up on his hands and feet and was scuttling backward, his bottom hanging beneath him, where it would be difficult to kick. "I should have helped you!"

"Oh? And you think this is a new idea to me?" Sir Lionel snapped, circling his brother, looking for an opening. "Guess what? I *always* thought you should have helped me, you blithering block!"

"Dash it, Lionel, I said I was wrong, didn't I?" Sir Lionel kicked him again, but again he missed the soft spot he was aiming for. "You always did fight dirty!" Sir Bors said.

"At least I fight," Sir Lionel rapped back, chasing his brother's beetling retreat.

While all this was going on, the hermit had picked himself up and dusted off his cloak. Now, staring furiously at Sir Lionel, he stepped between the brothers. "Stop!" he declared. "This man is my servant."

Sir Bors looked up from his bottom-defending crouch and said, "No, I'm not. This is my brother, the one I thought I'd killed."

166

The hermit looked sharply disappointed at this, but didn't give up. "No, it isn't!" he said. "It's . . . it's an apparition! A fiend from hell who has taken your brother's shape! Fiends can do that, you know."

Both knights stared at the hermit for a second; then Sir Bors rolled his eyes and said, "Shut up, you old poop."

Now Sir Lionel gaped at his brother. "Bors? Did you just call a religious man a . . . a poop?"

"Well, he *is!*" Bors said defensively. "You should have heard the twaddle he was trying to sell me before you came, trying to make me do his work for him."

"Oh, I don't deny his poopness," Sir Lionel said. "I'm just surprised to hear *you* admit it."

The hermit still stood between the brothers, towering over the crawling Sir Bors. Now he raised his arms in the air and said in a fierce voice, "Both of you are in grave danger at this moment."

Sir Lionel lifted one finger and poked the hermit in the chest. The holy man stepped backward, tripped over Sir Bors, and sat hard in the dirt. Sir Lionel extended his hand to his brother and said, "Why don't you get up, Bors? You look a proper ass crawling about like that."

Sir Bors took his brother's hand and, grinning, stood. Beaufils smiled. He'd never seen someone forgive his brother, but it was worth watching.

Unfortunately, the hermit was less impressed. Shaking

with fury, he rose to his feet. "It needed only this!" he rapped out. "No food in the larder, no wood for the fire, leaks in the roof, and chinks around the windows. Villagers dropping by day and night with their problems— 'Oh Mr. Hermit! Won't you tell me what to do with my rotten little boy?' As if I *cared!*" The hermit's voice was growing shrill. "And now I've been assaulted by a knight!"

"Assaulted?" repeated Sir Lionel.

"Assaulted, I tell you!"

"All I did was poke you in the chest." Sir Lionel glanced at Beaufils and Ellyn. "Do *you* think I assaulted him?"

"Well," Beaufils said thoughtfully, "he *does* have sensitive skin."

Ellyn began to giggle, and the hermit shrieked, "Now you're laughing at me! That's it! I'm done! Let somebody else have this hermitage, and see how they like it!" Struggling out of his hermit's robe, he threw it angrily on the ground and stomped down the trail away from the hut, wearing nothing but his linen underdrawers.

"Does this mean he's not holy anymore?" Beaufils asked.

"He's as holy as he ever was," Ellyn replied.

They camped that night at the now deserted hermitage, while Sir Bors and Ellyn tended to the cuts on Sir Lionel's back. Sir Bors and Sir Lionel had clearly forgotten their differences, and Beaufils enjoyed watching their banter and good-natured squabbling. Sir Bors was still the serious one, and Sir Lionel still the carefree one, and Beaufils reflected that he liked both of them more when the other was around than he did when they were alone.

Everything seemed to have worked out nicely for his two friends, but Sir Bors had one more test to face. Late that evening, after they had all been asleep for hours, a faint sound woke Beaufils. Ellyn was sleeping inside the hermitage, and Sir Lionel had stretched out at the far side of the clearing, but Beaufils and Sir Bors were sleeping in the yard before the hut, not far from the path, and Beaufils heard the unmistakable sound of a horse drawing near. He rose silently and slipped into the darkest shadows just before the horse entered the clearing.

The horse stopped, and Beaufils could make out the black outline of its rider against the gray sky: it was a woman. Sir Bors stirred, then sat up in his blankets. "Who's there?" he said in a husky whisper.

The rider sighed mournfully and said, "A poor destitute woman who has been cast from her childhood home and left to roam the darkness, prey to every danger that awaits a friendless female."

"I know that voice," Sir Bors said slowly. "Lady Orgille?"

"Sir Bors?"

"So Erskine kicked you out of the castle, did he? I thought he would."

Lady Orgille dropped from the saddle, walked over to where the knight lay, and knelt beside his prone form. "It was horrible!" she said, her voice cracking. "That man threw me from my home, giving me nothing."

"Looks like he gave you a horse, at least," commented Sir Bors, who was edging away from Lady Orgille.

She leaned closer. "But I would have left the castle anyway, dear Sir Bors," she said. "When you rode away this afternoon, I watched you go and my heart broke in my bosom, and I knew that I would never be happy without you and your love. That's why I'm here. I've come looking for you."

"Have you, then?" Sir Bors said. His voice was flat.

"Could you . . . could you ever forgive me and take me back? I could ask no greater happiness than to ride at your side, to care for you, to sleep in the warmth of your presence, to—"

She got no further. Sir Bors rose abruptly and nearly dragged Lady Orgille by the wrist back to her horse. "Get up," he said.

"Sir Bors!"

Setting both hands on Lady Orgille's waist, Sir Bors practically threw her up into the saddle. "Off you go."

"Sir Bors, don't you . . . don't you think I'm beautiful?"

170

Sir Bors looked at her in the moonlight for a second. "No," he said at last. "You only look like it. Now get out of here, you viper." Then Sir Bors slapped Lady Orgille's horse in the haunches, startling it into a gallop. He watched until the horse's shadow had been swallowed up by the larger darkness and the last echo of its hooves had died away, then returned to his blankets and rolled up in them. Beaufils watched from the shadows, grinning.

"Damn, that felt good," Sir Bors muttered as he went back to sleep.

IX

THE BLOOD OF A MAIDEN

"You know what bothers me?" Ellyn asked suddenly. She and Beaufils had separated from Sir Bors and Lionel that morning and for the past several hours had been riding over a dry plain in companionable silence, both lost in their own thoughts.

"No. What bothers you?"

"Lady Orgille."

"Oh, her," Beaufils said. "I didn't like her much myself."

"I just can't believe a woman would do that!"

"Do what?"

"Use people like that." Ellyn glanced at Beaufils's puzzled expression, then laughed shortly. "I know you don't know what I mean. As I said before, you're different from most men, probably because you didn't know

172

any others when you were growing up. The thing is, normally when you find someone using other people as tools to get what they want, it'll be a man."

Beaufils thought about this for a moment. It seemed strange to him. "And women don't use other people?"

Ellyn hesitated at that. "Not like men do, anyway. That's why Lady Orgille bothers me. She acts like a *man*."

This still sounded odd to Beaufils, but he decided to let it go. Ellyn sounded very intense, especially the way she said *man*, and he had learned from his time with Galahad that it was just when people were most intense that you could get the least sense from them.

Ellyn muttered, half to herself, "I wish sometimes I could go to a land where there were only women."

Beaufils glanced around them at the brown grass and stunted trees through which they were riding. "Well," he commented, "maybe we'll find such a place. I doubt it's around here, though. Not much life at all in these parts."

It did seem that the farther they rode, the more barren the landscape became. They had left behind all that was green and fresh. As far as they could see, fields of wispy brown grass were interrupted only by small, jagged, unhealthy trees with only a few brown and yellow leaves clinging in forlorn bunches to the limbs. Before long, the grass itself began to thin, leaving dusty, bare patches. Within an hour they were trotting through sand and rock and hard, cracked dirt.

"This can't be right," Ellyn said at last.

Beaufils examined the barren waste. The land seemed dead, but it was somehow beautiful too. Without any vegetation around to distract the eye, the rocks and dirt seemed to stand out more proudly, revealing their true selves. "Let's keep going, though. I've never been in a place like this."

"Neither has anyone else," muttered Ellyn. "At least let's rest the animals and walk a bit."

So they dismounted and began plodding through the arid land. There was no sign of life, but the air tasted somehow cleaner and purer here, like spring water. Beaufils found himself taking it in with deep breaths. He was measuring his breathing with his paces—about four steps for each breath in and five for each breath out—when he became suddenly aware that they were not alone. Ellyn was still walking quietly at his left, but at his right, as if he had materialized from nowhere, strode a young man. So sudden was his appearance and so silent his movement that Beaufils thought at first he was imagining him. Then the stranger turned his head and smiled.

"Ellyn?" Beaufils said, slowing his pace.

"Yes?" Ellyn said, glancing his way. Then she gave a startled yelp.

"Oh, good," Beaufils said. "You see him, too." He stopped. "Good morning, man."

"Good morning, Beaufils. Good morning, Lady Ellyn," the man replied. Now that Beaufils was looking more closely at their sudden companion, he was no longer sure that he was young. His face was smooth and unlined, and his easy smile had a youthful feel to it, but his eyes seemed far older than his face. "Sorry if I gave you a start," he said. "You seemed to be enjoying the walk, and I didn't want to disturb you."

"How do you know our names?" Beaufils asked.

"I've come especially to find you," the stranger said. "My name's Terence."

The name was familiar, and Beaufils searched his memory. "Aren't you . . . Gawain's . . . something?"

"Yes, I'm Gawain's squire," Terence said.

"You're a squire?" Ellyn said, incredulously, staring at Terence's curiously ancient eyes. "You don't *look* like a servant. More like a prince."

"Can't a fellow be more than one thing?" Terence asked mildly. Then he looked at Beaufils. "Tell me, Beaufils. How's your quest going?"

"We haven't seen the Grail, if that's what you mean."

"It wasn't, but that's all right. Now that I get a good look at you, I can see you're doing well." He looked across at Ellyn. "And you? Have you found what you're looking for, Lady Ellyn?"

175

"I don't know that I'm looking for anything at all," she said. "I didn't really come on this quest to find that Grail thing. I just wanted to see the world."

"Especially the parts where there are no men," Beaufils commented.

Ellyn blushed and cast a reproachful look at Beaufils, but Terence only nodded and said, "Like the Castles of Women?"

"Castles of Women? Places where there are no men?" Ellyn asked

"Yes. Castles and islands where no man is allowed. But I ought to tell you that ladies who go there just to get away from men don't usually stay."

"Where are these castles?"

"Most of them are in the Other World," Terence said.

"What do you mean, 'Other World'?" asked Beaufils curiously.

Terence indicated with a nod that that they should start walking again, and once they were moving he said, "There is another world beyond the one we can see."

Ellyn frowned skeptically, but Beaufils asked, "Only one?"

Terence smiled suddenly, with clear pleasure. "Do you know, Beaufils, you are the first person who has ever asked me that question. Usually people have trouble believing in *any* world other than their own, let alone many. But you're right. There are a great many worlds, more than any of us know."

"I've often wondered," Beaufils said. "Tell me about this other one."

"The one I mean is the World of Faeries," Terence said.

"Do you mean the World of Faeries or Faery Tale World?" Ellyn asked scornfully.

"I'm not sure it makes any difference," Terence replied. "But if you're suggesting that this world exists *only* in the imagination of storytellers, you're wrong. It does exist in stories, but that makes it no less real. Anyway, that's why I'm here. You're about to enter that world, and I've been sent to show you to the crossing."

Beaufils was delighted, as if he'd been longing all his life to go to this world but hadn't known it until this moment. "When do we go?" he asked.

"The crossing is just past those sandhills," Terence replied. "If Lady Ellyn is willing."

Ellyn still looked dubious. "Forgive me, Squire Terence, but can you give me any reason to trust you?"

"There's never a reason to trust someone," Terence said. "If there's a reason, then it's not trust."

"I trust him," Beaufils said.

Ellyn hesitated again, and for several moments her doubts played across her face. Then she sighed and said, "I don't know that I do trust you, Squire Terence, but I trust Beaufils."

"That should be enough," Terence replied with a smile. "This way." He led them on a faint trail between high mounds of loose sand. "When you've made the crossing, you'll be in the World of Faeries. Don't worry. It isn't that different from here, barring the occasional ogre. Once there, you must go wherever Lady Ellyn says."

"Me?" Ellyn demanded.

"Yes. For now, at least, you'll be following Lady Ellyn's quest." Terence led them past the last dune, and they found themselves in a warm, brackish stream, no deeper than the tops of their feet.

"*My* quest?" Ellyn said. "But what *is* my quest?"

Terence, who had remained behind them on the bank, only said, "It would be helpful to figure that out, Lady Ellyn," and then the ground sank beneath them, and the water rose up their bodies and covered their heads. Beaufils sensed Ellyn thrashing about in fear beside him, and reaching over, he took her arm. Then they and their horses were climbing out of a clear blue pool in a forest glade, with snow-capped mountains standing behind them. The wasteland and Terence were gone.

Ellyn sputtered and coughed, then said vehemently, "I *hate* getting water up my nose!"

Terence had been right. Except for being in a lush green forest instead of a barren waste, there didn't seem to be much difference between the two worlds. The plants and insects that surrounded them were the same ones they would have seen in a forest in their own world, and as Beaufils pointed out, there wasn't even one ogre.

"Well, don't sound so disappointed," Ellyn said.

"But I've never seen one," Beaufils said wistfully.

"A body doesn't have to see everything," Ellyn muttered. She put her hands on her hips and looked around them in all directions, then said, "If we've all had enough to drink, let's go that way."

"Fine with me. You're the leader," Beaufils said.

This made Ellyn smile, and she mounted her horse and set off at a good clip, so that Clover had to trot to catch up. They rode through a perfumed evergreen forest, across a mountain meadow filled with flowers, then down a long slope of springy bracken. Through all this they saw no sign of other people, but then they came upon a knight in a field.

They saw the knight before he saw them. He was on a white horse on a small knoll, looking down a long slope into a valley. He wore full armor, of flashing silver. His visor hid his face, but Beaufils had no trouble identifying him. "Galahad!" he exclaimed with mild pleasure.

179

Galahad turned his horse, drawing his sword very swiftly indeed and facing them in grim silence as they approached. "Do we have to?" muttered Ellyn.

"I know you don't care for him," Beaufils said, "but he's an old friend. We don't have to ride with him, but I can't just ignore him. He's not a bad fellow, after all."

As they drew near, Galahad's tense figure relaxed slightly, but when they were only ten yards or so away, he called out, "Halt!"

Beaufils and Ellyn stopped. "Hello, Galahad," said Beaufils, "What brings you here?"

"What is your name?" Galahad demanded.

"Have you forgotten?" Beaufils asked. "It's Beaufils."

"And who is that woman at your side?"

"You haven't had a knock on the head, have you?" Beaufils asked. "Once that happened to me when I was young. Fell out of a tree on my head, and Mother told me that for several hours I couldn't remember anything. I got better, though," he added encouragingly.

"I'm Lady Ellyn of Carlisle," Ellyn said. "You stayed at my father's castle."

"I remember your faces and names," Galahad said grimly. "But I still do not know you. How do I know you are not fiends who have taken human shape to tempt me?"

"Trust me," Ellyn said. "There's nothing I want to do less than tempt you."

"That's just what a fiend would say," Galahad replied.

Ellyn glanced at Beaufils. "You're right. He's had a knock on the head."

"Tell me how I came to know you, Beaufils—if that's *really* your name," Galahad demanded.

"Well, that's sort of the problem, isn't it? I don't know if it *is* really my name. That's why I went with you to Camelot: I wanted to find my father and ask. That was when we met in the forest. You were with that nasty fellow Mordred, who tried to kill—"

"A fiend would still know all this!"

Ellyn tugged on Beaufils's sleeve. "Come on, Beau. Your friend Galahad wants to be alone."

"I do *not* want to be alone," Galahad replied belligerently.

"Well, then, I want you to be alone," Ellyn snapped back. "Come *on*, Beau."

"Wait!" Galahad said. "What if you aren't fiends but angels sent to guide me? Then I would be making a grave error in not receiving you."

Ellyn rolled her eyes. "Lord, help us," she muttered.

At Ellyn's words Galahad relaxed. "Beaufils! It *is* you! How wonderful to see you again." Beaufils and Ellyn glanced at each other in confusion, but Galahad explained, "No fiend could say, 'Lord, help us.' Now I know you are who you say and have come to aid my quest."

"Blast," Ellyn said under her breath.

"I'd be happy to help if I can," Beaufils said, "but actually Ellyn and I are on a different quest this time—Ellyn's quest."

"What quest is that?"

"We don't know yet," Beaufils replied with a smile. "I'm hoping we'll recognize it when we find it."

"Do you know where to look?" Galahad asked.

"No."

"Then we can ride together," Galahad said. "After all, I don't know where I'm going, either. Why shouldn't we go in the same direction? Say, do you know where we are?"

Beaufils hesitated. He was remembering that with Galahad you had to be careful how much to say, because he didn't like to hear things that didn't go along with what he already thought. "Sort of," he said. "How did you get here?"

"I came upon a strange boat in a great river. It had no pilot or crew, but on its deck there was a bed with carved pillars and damask curtains and this ancient sword sheath." He showed them a sheath of black leather that hung at his side. "I rode on board to see this wonder, and the boat left the shore. It crossed a great sea and brought me to this place. Are we in France?"

"I don't think so," Beaufils said carefully.

"Where, then?"

There was nothing else for it. "Well, we were told that this is the World of Faeries."

"Faeries!" Galahad exclaimed. Beaufils nodded, and Galahad gripped his sword more tightly. "I *knew* this was a devilish place. Let us ride on and meet the adventure that comes."

He started down the slope, but Beaufils stopped him. "Er, Galahad, there's one thing. On Ellyn's quest, we are to go only where Ellyn leads. You don't mind letting her pick our way, do you?"

"Let a woman lead?"

"Let Ellyn lead, yes."

"What sort of quest can be led by a woman?"

Ellyn, who had sat in brooding silence during this whole exchange, spoke suddenly. "*My* quest. That's what sort."

Galahad threw back his shoulders. "I am on a man's quest," he said. "I cannot follow a female."

Ellyn straightened her own back. "Well, I'm on a *woman's* quest, and I'd just as soon that you didn't—"

"Who do you suppose those fellows are?" Beaufils asked. Galahad and Ellyn both looked at him, then followed his gaze down the hill, where a line of nearly ten knights rode toward them, each holding a lance.

"Don't worry, Lady Ellyn," Galahad said. "I'll protect you."

"I don't need your protection!" Ellyn snapped.

"Not much you could do anyway," Beaufils pointed out to Galahad. "Ten knights with lances against three people without them. And you're the only one with a sword and armor."

By now the knights had drawn near, and the line curved around them, forming a circle. Then they pointed their lances at the three. One of the knights spoke loudly. "Is that a maiden?"

Galahad and Ellyn maintained a rigid silence, so after a few seconds Beaufils said, "You can't tell? Do you not have many women hereabouts? I mean, they *do* have a pretty distinctive—"

"Are you a maiden?" the knight rapped out.

"Last time I checked, yes," Ellyn said.

"You will come with us!" the knight replied. "All of you."

"In here!" declared the knight, opening a great oaken door at the end of the long hall.

The troop of knights had led them into the valley, along a river, around a great rocky crag, and to a massive stone castle, built, so it seemed, right into the side of a mountain. A drawbridge had lowered, and they had crossed the river into a cavernous courtyard. There the knights had disarmed Galahad, then conducted them all down the dim hallway at swordpoint.

"This," the head knight added, "is the chamber of our mistress, ruler of these lands, the Lady Petunia."

The three companions stepped into a room that was brightly lit by torches and a vast fireplace, then all stopped involuntarily. Ellyn gasped, and Galahad muttered a quick prayer under his breath. Beaufils only nodded slowly. "Oh," he said. "This is why you weren't sure what a maiden looked like."

The woman who lay on the monstrous bed in the center of the room was as foul a creature as Beaufils had ever seen. She was vast and flaccid, and where her skin showed, it was swollen and puffy. Her face was mottled gray and red and raddled with pustules, many of which were oozing a clear fluid that formed patches of flaking, yellow crust. Her hair, what little there was of it, was wispy and wild and incongruously bedecked with dainty pink bows and ribbons. Small, beady black eyes looked out from behind puffy cheeks and bushy eyebrows. Judging from the shape beneath the sheets, the Lady Petunia was easily twice as large as any woman Beaufils had ever seen. A foul odor filled the room.

"My dear lady," said the head knight, bowing. "We have found a maiden!"

"Oh, you're so good to me, dear, dear Ronnie," Lady Petunia said to the knight. Her voice was surprisingly shrill and thin, almost girlish, for one of her bulk.

"What would I ever do without such loyal, loving knights?"

"It is my honor to serve you, my lady."

"But you do so much," the woman said, her voice cracking as if she were about to cry. "I don't deserve such service, an old woman like me who is not long for this world."

"You must not say so, my dear!" the knight said earnestly, kneeling beside the bed. "You see, I've brought the maiden for the cure! The last one we need, too!"

"Ronnie!" the lady said sharply. "Mind your tongue!"

The knight looked stricken. "I'm sorry! Oh, my lady, I'm such a fool! My wretched—"

"There, there, Ronnie," the woman said soothingly. "You know I can never be angry with my dear boys for long. You will learn. I don't suppose you could . . . no, you've done far too much already."

"How can I serve you?"

Lady Petunia looked at a plate covered with crumbs that lay beside her on the bed. "That silly manservant has let my bonbon plate go all empty."

The knight rose to his feet instantly. "I shall speak to the churl at once!"

"Now, Ronnie, don't be harsh with the poor boy," Lady Petunia said. "You know how difficult it must be for a pretty young man like that to serve an ugly hag like me."

"He cannot have said so!"

"It doesn't really matter if he did," Lady Petunia said, her voice becoming fainter. "It's only the truth, after all. I'm sure you will all be much happier when I die."

"I shall cut out his tongue for saying such things!" the knight exclaimed, livid with rage.

"But then who will bring me my bonbons?" Lady Petunia said plaintively.

"I shall bring them myself!"

With that, the knight stormed from the room, murder in his eyes, while Lady Petunia turned her black eyes on the three visitors. "Oh, my!" she said, looking from Galahad to Beaufils and back. "What pretty, pretty young men!" She blinked a few times and made a grimace that Beaufils guessed was supposed to be a smile. Then she looked at Ellyn, and her eyes grew cold. "And a pretty girl as well. You *do* think you're pretty, don't you, girl?"

Ellyn's voice was hoarse, but she said, "That's not really for me to say, my lady."

"Now, now, let's not play games," Lady Petunia said. "You are a beautiful girl, and you know it. You remind me of myself at your age." She gave a mournful sigh, while all three visitors stared at her with incredulity. "Indeed, I think I may have had the edge on you in my day," Lady Petunia continued, "but that day is long past, I'm afraid. Now I suppose all my knights will be falling in love with you and ignoring me, leaving me here all alone to die. Oh well, it's no more than I expect."

With what seemed to be her last ounce of energy, she pulled a cloth rope that hung by her bed, and at once a door opened and a man of middle years hurried into the room. "Dear, dear Eggie-poo," Lady Petunia said. "Were you just waiting for my bell? Oh, you mustn't do that. I know you have better things to do than to serve an old wreck like me."

The man knelt in abject subservience. "I live but to serve you, my dear."

Lady Petunia fluttered her swollen eyelids again. "So silly of you," she murmured faintly. "As if I were worth such loyalty. But if you *do* want to help me, you could take these visitors to the guest hall and explain things to them."

"At once, my precious lady," Eggie-poo said. Then he rose and led the three out of Lady Petunia's room.

"I am Sir Egbert," the man said once they were in a spacious, though ill-lit, room with several bedchambers branching off from it.

"Not Eggie-poo?" Beaufils asked.

The man's jaw clenched momentarily, then relaxed. "My lady," he said, "is not well."

"Really?" Ellyn said politely.

"She has been grievously afflicted by a horrid

enchantment, thrown on her by an evil man named Ganscotter."

"Ganscotter," Beaufils repeated softly.

"The curse was meant to destroy her, but my mistress is an enchantress herself, and by her own arts she has discovered that one thing alone may prevent her death." Then he hesitated, avoiding the gaze of all three.

"Yes?" asked Galahad. "What is this?"

"Only the blood of a maiden," Sir Egbert said.

"Oh," they all said together. Beaufils and Galahad looked at Ellyn.

"Er, how much blood?" asked Beaufils.

"One small bowl," Sir Egbert said hurriedly. "We should be very careful not to hurt you, my lady. Just a pinprick in the arm, and we'd make you very easy while we bled you."

Ellyn looked at him suspiciously and said, "Why go to all that bother? After all, we're your prisoners, aren't we? You could just kill me and take all the blood you want."

Sir Egbert winced. "Please, my lady, let us not talk about killing. No one wants to kill you. But the thing is, the blood cannot be taken by force. It must be given willingly or it will have no healing power."

Ellyn and Beaufils looked at each other, eyes wide. Sir Egbert bowed and, seemingly in a hurry, excused himself from the room. "You'll want to discuss this among yourselves," he said. "I shall be back shortly." Then he left, closing the door behind him.

Before Beaufils or Ellyn could speak, Galahad burst out, "But this must be it!"

"Must be what?" asked Ellyn.

"Your quest, of course! I did not understand how a woman could have a quest, but now I see it all clearly. The quest of womanhood is the quest of self-sacrifice!"

"Bosh," Ellyn retorted.

"A woman gives herself for the sake of others, for her children, for her husband, for all! It is the noblest part of womanhood! My own mother, the most virtuous of all women, gave everything for me. No sacrifice was too great for her to bear. She never denied me anything!"

"Unfortunate child," Ellyn murmured.

"What could be more perfect a quest for a fair lady?" Galahad demanded. "To give of the lifeblood that flows through her veins so another can live! It is a perfect symbol of womanhood! Do you not think it noble to save another's life?"

Ellyn hesitated. "Yes, I suppose it is. All things considered, though, I'd rather my lifeblood went to save a different life than Lady Petunia's."

Beaufils nodded. "Appalling, wasn't she? I think maybe I'm finally starting to understand the difference between beautiful and ugly. That was ugly, wasn't it?"

"Yes, it was," Ellyn replied, "and not just her appearance, either."

"It ill becomes you to insult a helpless woman thus," Galahad said austerely.

"Helpless?" Ellyn repeated. "There was nothing helpless about Lady Petunia. She had everyone dancing to her will."

"Yes," Beaufils said. "I wondered about that, because you said earlier today that women don't use other people as tools, but I thought Lady Petunia—"

"I may have to rethink that," Ellyn replied hastily. "A nasty piece of work, wasn't she?"

Galahad broke in. "It little matters whether you like the woman or not. Is it yours to decide if she deserves to live?"

Ellyn glanced at Beaufils. "True," she said. "For once, your annoying friend is right." Then she looked back at Galahad. "But has it occurred to you that I might die?"

"I thought about that," Beaufils said. "I wonder how big this bowl is."

"What if you do die?" Galahad demanded. "What could be more noble than to lay down your life for another? I promise you, Lady Ellyn, that if you die in this endeavor, I shall honor you as long as I live."

"Thank you," Ellyn said. "That will be a great comfort, I'm sure." She shook her head as if to clear it, then said, "I need to think alone for a while." Going into one of the bedchambers, she closed the door.

Galahad gazed at the closed door for a long moment, then let out a sigh and said, "Yes. Now I understand. I must learn to think of others before myself. Lady Ellyn's sacrifice is showing me the way."

Beaufils frowned and, when Galahad said nothing more, commented, "I'm sure that's an excellent lesson, Galahad, but I say, now that you've learned it, perhaps Ellyn doesn't need to risk her life after all."

But Galahad ignored him, caught up in his own meditations, and after waiting a frustrating moment for a reply, Beaufils turned on his heel and went out into the hall.

It was deserted, and Beaufils walked down the corridor, thinking how odd it was that anyone should build a castle underground, where there could be no windows. The only light was artificial, mostly from tiny candles that guttered in occasional sconces along the hallway. He looked in each room he passed, finding each one empty and somehow darker and more oppressive than the one before. At last he came to the final candle, but the hall continued on, a black pit yawning before him, leading into the mountain. "Where?" Beaufils muttered to himself, and his voice seemed eerily loud.

Taking the last candle from its sconce, Beaufils

walked into the blackness, feeling the thick darkness open before him, then fold behind him when he had passed. He could not explain why he felt the need to plunge into this sea of hiddenness, but his steps did not falter as he pressed on down the hall to whatever awaited him in the sunless depths. Finally he came to the end of the corridor, and without hesitating he pushed open the closed door that he found there.

The tiny candle flickered, and the small circle of light that it gave seemed to contract. The pungent and offensive smell of decaying meat met Beaufils's nostrils, but he stepped over the threshold and into the room. A sense that went beyond sight told him that he was in a vast room with a high ceiling, and the dim glow of his candle revealed a stone shelf built into the wall on his left. On the shelf lay a skeleton. Beaufils stepped near and looked more closely. From the dress of fine linen that still covered the skeleton and the long wisps of hair that lay about the grinning skull, he could tell that this had once been a woman. Lifting his eyes, he made out the gray form of another skeleton, on another shelf a few steps farther along. He began to walk around the perimeter of the room, finding another skeleton every ten feet or so. All were laid out with care, their arms across their chests; all were women. After he had passed a dozen skeletons, the smell of decay grew stronger, and he realized that he was now passing bodies that had not wholly rotted away. Now he could see on the bones bits of crumbling flesh. Beaufils felt a wave of nausea, and he picked up his pace, passing several more corpses quickly. At the end of the row, though, he stopped, for the last body was so recently dead that it was still whole. This had been a young woman, and had the body not been so pale and white it would have appeared to be merely a young woman sleeping. Stretching out his candle, Beaufils looked closely at the face, then at an arm. There, at the crook of the elbow, was a hole surrounded by an ugly bruise.

"And did you give your lifeblood willingly?" he asked in a whisper. He stepped back until he was in the center of the room, then held his candle high and looked around. He remembered that back in his forest home, before he had set out, the old man had told him that in the world he would find much wickedness. "Yes," Beaufils said sadly. "More wickedness than I could have imagined." His head felt very heavy, and he allowed it to sink to his chin for a moment, but then he raised it. "Sleep well, sisters," he said hoarsely. "Perhaps you have already come to a kinder world." He looked back at the last body and realized that he had walked almost all the way around the room and had returned to the door through which he had entered. Between the last corpse and the doorway there was only one more stone slab, awaiting one more body. His eyes widened as he remember what the knight called Ronnie had said when he had ushered Ellyn in to Lady Petunia: *I've brought the maiden for the cure; the last one we need, too.* Turning on his heel, Beaufils ran back down the corridor, holding his candle before him like a sword, cutting the blackness as he returned to the world of the living.

When he came back to the guest hall where he had left the others, the rooms were empty. Filled with sudden panic, he threw his candle aside and began to run back down the hall toward Lady Petunia's chamber. As he approached the door, he saw two armed guards—one of them the knight Ronnie—standing outside.

"You may not enter!" Ronnie said.

"You can't stop me," replied Beaufils quickly. Ronnie drew his sword, and Beaufils took it away from him. He was not sure exactly how he did so, because he acted entirely on instinct, but at one instant Ronnie had had a sword, and in the next instant Beaufils had twisted it from his grasp and was holding the point at the other guard's throat. "I have looked on the face of death today," Beaufils said quietly. "I don't wish to cause it."

"I have sworn to my mistress that I will protect this room," Ronnie said tensely. Then he leaped forward, and Beaufils flicked the sword away from the other guard's throat and thrust it forward at Ronnie. It was not by conscious design, but the point of the sword slipped between two armor plates just at the bend of Ronnie's left arm, in the exact spot where Beaufils had seen the wound in the arm of the last corpse. Blood spurted through the armor, and Beaufils turned to the other guard. "Bind up his arm!" he snapped. The guard hesitated, and Beaufils added, "Help someone to live, not to die!"

The guard knelt by Ronnie, and Beaufils threw aside the sword and pushed open the door to Lady Petunia's chamber. There was Ellyn, standing before the lady's vast bed, with Galahad just off to the side, near a strange man who held a knife and a large bowl. Beaufils drew a breath to shout a warning to Ellyn, but before he made a sound, he heard Ellyn say, in a clear voice, "No!"

"No?" Lady Petunia wheezed. "Are you going to be so selfish? Are you so unnatural a female as to put herself before others?"

"I will not give my blood for you to live, my lady."

"Then your guilt will weigh on your head forever. How will you sleep at night? Can you deny your very nature? What is woman apart from self-giving love? Nothing! Nothing!" Lady Petunia's face was turning alarmingly purple.

"Lady Ellyn," said Galahad, stepping forward. "Think what you are doing! Can you not give of yourself to help another?"

"Selfish! Selfish!" Lady Petunia shrieked. "Oh, that I

should have lived long enough to see so foul and unnatural a woman!"

Ellyn gritted her teeth, but she replied clearly, "Lady Petunia, one day I may give my life for another, but if that happens it will be out of love, not out of duty and certainly not just because I'm female."

Lady Petunia's eyes bulged, and she began to gabble incoherently. Flailing with her arms, she pushed her massive form to a sitting position, and then, quite suddenly, fell back on the pillows and was silent. The man who had been holding the knife and basin threw them down and rushed to the bed. "My lady! My lady!" he exclaimed. For several minutes he felt for her heartbeat, and then he sank slowly to his knees beside the bed. "My lady!" he said again, brokenly.

"You have caused a woman's death, Lady Ellyn!" Galahad said sternly.

"No," Beaufils said. "Lady Petunia caused her own death." He stepped forward and touched the kneeling man's shoulder. The man looked up, his eyes wet, and Beaufils said, "Lay her on the last slab in the hall of death. Put her beside all the maidens who died for her."

The man looked up blankly, then nodded.

"What maidens?" asked Ellyn.

Before Beaufils could reply, a dull blue light began to shine from Lady Petunia's body. As they watched, the glow formed a swaddling band about the corpse, and in the midst of the light, Lady Petunia began to change. The raddled skin knit itself together and grew smooth. The puffiness around the eyes subsided, the wispy hair thickened, and the body's huge dimensions shrank. A minute later, they were staring at a different person, a pleasantly plump woman of middle years, with lustrous gray hair, a few fine wrinkles beside her eyes, and an amiable expression on her dead face. In the shape of the face, though, there was still something familiar.

The man who had held the basin caught his breath and said, "Mother!"

"Mother?" Beaufils asked.

"This is what she used to look like, what she was supposed to become again once we had filled the hall of maidens. Mother promised it would be so."

"She is your mother?" Ellyn repeated.

"All of us in this castle are her children," the man said simply. "We would have given our souls for her."

"You did," Beaufils said. He took Ellyn's arm and began leading her away. He looked once over his shoulder at the man. "Your mother was once very beautiful." Then, leaving by a different door than the one Beaufils had pushed open a few minutes earlier, the two withdrew from the room, followed by Galahad, and together they found their way to the stables, where their mounts awaited.

X

A Kiss for the Dragon

Beaufils and Galahad rode along the river, behind Ellyn.
None of them spoke. Beaufils, for his part, was too
weary to talk. His journey to the death hall had taken
something out of him—something more than mere
strength. It was as if he had left some vital part of his
soul behind, beside the bodies on the stone shelves, and
his thoughts were never far from the maidens he had
found there. Ellyn also seemed exhausted, and as for
Galahad, he was clearly struggling with a strong sense
of shock and indignation.

At last Galahad put his feelings into words. "You let
that woman die," he said to Ellyn.

"Yes, I did," she replied in a toneless voice.

"How *could* you?"

Beaufils judged it time to intervene. "Before you

answer, Ellyn, I need to tell you both something." Then he described what he had found in the hall of maidens. "So you see, Lady Petunia and her sons knew from the beginning that Ellyn would die, just like all the others."

Ellyn stared at Beaufils, her face stricken, her eyes filled with horror. "Oh, Beau," she whispered. "All those girls. And you found them lying there? How . . . are you all right?"

"All right, yes. But different," Beaufils said. "And you? You had to make a horrible choice. How are you?"

"As you said, different. I'll recover, but I won't be the same."

Galahad broke in. "I don't think it makes any difference at all. Yes, it was very wrong of them to kill all those girls—though we need to remember that they gave their lives willingly—but it doesn't change anything for Lady Ellyn. She didn't know about those noble girls when she refused Lady Petunia."

"But it did make a difference," Beaufils pointed out. "When Ellyn refused, Lady Petunia was restored. She became who she was supposed to be, a gentle old woman."

"She may have looked better, but she was still dead!"

"That's the only thing that *didn't* change," Beaufils said. "Lady Petunia was dead already. That whole castle was. Now maybe some of her sons can leave that horrible place. By the way, have you wondered why

200

they were all sons? Didn't she have any daughters? What happened to them?"

Galahad shook his head. "It makes no difference," he said doggedly. "Killing her was a mortal sin, and I only hope we find a priest soon for Lady Ellyn to make confession to."

Ellyn abandoned the dispute wearily. Beaufils, considering Galahad's last words, was wondering idly if there *were* any priests in the World of Faeries when they rode through a stand of trees into a small clearing, in the center of which was a tiny log house. "A hermitage!" Galahad declared joyously, flinging himself from his horse and hurrying toward the hut.

"I really, really don't feel like meeting a hermit just now," Ellyn murmured.

"Not all holy men are annoying," Beaufils reminded her. "Remember the good Basil. Say, why's Galahad stopping?"

Galahad had halted his run forward and now was standing hesitantly in the little yard, staring at the hut.

"There's no door," Ellyn said suddenly. "Just that one shuttered window." Galahad started forward again and walked all around the cabin. "Is there one on the other side?" Ellyn asked him.

Galahad shook his head, then leaned toward the window. "Father?" he asked uncertainly.

The shutters opened and a smiling face appeared.

"You can call me Father if you like, but if you really want to be accurate, you should find another title." It was a woman.

"I know who you are!" Galahad burst out suddenly.

"Do you?" the woman replied. "That will save time on introductions. But you'll still have to tell me who you are."

"You are an anchoress!" Galahad exclaimed.

"Yes, I am," she replied. "But that isn't *who* I am, only what. My name is Irena. And what are your names?"

Galahad ignored the question. "God be praised!" he murmured, sinking to his knees and raising his eyes toward the sky. "For leading us to this holy place!"

Ellyn slipped easily from her horse and walked over to the cabin. "My name is Ellyn," she said. "This is my friend Le Beau Desconus and my traveling companion Sir Galahad."

"I'm very glad to meet you all," Irena replied, and from the smile in her eyes Beaufils saw that she meant it.

"What is an anchoress?" he asked, dismounting and joining Galahad and Ellyn by the window.

Irena looked surprised. "You've never heard of anchoresses?"

"I had a sheltered childhood," Beaufils explained. "It gave me a late start."

"An anchoress," Irena explained, "is a woman who goes apart from society and lives in a cell, like this one, devoting herself to prayer. Sort of a female hermit. Do you know about hermits?"

"Oh, yes," Ellyn replied. "We've met a lot of hermits."

"Hmm," Irena replied. "By your tone, I gather that you didn't enjoy them all."

"Not all of them, no," Beaufils admitted. "It was back in the World of Men. Do you know that world?"

"I'm from there myself," Irena said.

"Oh, then have you heard of a place called the Sacred Forest?"

"Dear me, yes," Irena replied, shaking her head sadly. "I understand you now. A dreary place, the Sacred Forest. I don't suppose you met . . . anyone there you *did* like, did you?"

"Yes," Beaufils said. "A hermit named Basil."

Irena smiled broadly. "Oh, good. You found him. Dear Basil. Is he well?"

"Very well, thank you," Beaufils replied politely.

Ellyn had stood through this exchange with a frown deepening on her face. "I'm sorry to interrupt," she said. "But did you really *choose* to live in this tiny log hovel?"

"I did, yes, and I do."

"How can you do that? How do you get out?"

"I don't," Irena replied.

"How do you eat?"

"The people who live nearby bring me food, far more than I need."

"They bring you food? Why?"

Irena smiled. "I think they have some notion that I pray for them in return for their gifts. Silly of them, really, but I've stopped trying to argue."

Ellyn raised her eyebrows. "What do you mean, 'silly'?" she asked.

"They ought to know that I would pray for them whether they brought me food or not, but I'm afraid some people have a terrible time believing in gifts."

Ellyn shook her head again. "But this looks like a prison!"

Irena looked mildly at Ellyn for a moment before answering. "And I?" she said at last. "Do I look like a prisoner?"

Ellyn seemed confused by the question, so after a moment Beaufils answered. "No, Irena. You don't."

Irena acknowledged his reply with a nod, but she kept her eyes on Ellyn. "And have you never seen anyone who lived at liberty in a great palace who *did* seem like a prisoner?"

"Yes," Ellyn said softly. "In fact, we've just come from a place like that—a magnificent castle filled with people in bondage."

"When you know what a prison is really like, then you will find what you seek."

Beaufils didn't understand this, but he had a sense that it wouldn't do any good to ask for an explanation.

He wouldn't have had time anyway, because just then Galahad, who had been gazing rapturously all this time at the sky and ignoring everything that was being said, rose to his feet. "My lady," he said. "I honor you."

"That's very kind of you, child," Irena replied. "But you don't have to, you know."

"Such true womanliness!" Galahad declared, giving Ellyn a disdainful glance. "To devote your life to prayer and purity! To sacrifice yourself and all your happiness for the sake of others."

"Oh, I'm quite happy," Irena said. "I don't feel that I'm making a sacrifice at all."

"You are so brave!" Galahad said reverently.

Irena sighed. "Yes, of course. Quite." Her eyes met Ellyn's, then crinkled with amusement. "He means well, you know," she said softly.

Ignoring her words, Galahad announced, "I only hope that this lady with whom I ride can learn something from your example!"

"Yes, I hope that, too," Irena said. She smiled at Ellyn. "But I'm not worried about it. You will find your joy, dear."

Galahad returned to his horse and mounted. "We have been inspired to have been with you."

"And likewise, I'm sure," Irena murmured. "And, if you're looking for a place to stay this evening, let me suggest you follow the river downstream a few miles to the castle of Lady Synadona. Perhaps you could even help her with a problem or two. You must insist on seeing Lady Synadona personally, though."

With that, Irena smiled again, then closed the shutters and returned to her dark cell. Beaufils and Ellyn glanced at each other, then mounted and joined Galahad in riding toward the river.

"That's a castle?" Beaufils asked, delighted with the sight that lay before him. The castle of Lady Synadona was unlike any he'd seen. The walls were of stone, but not of rough and jagged stone like the castles he had seen in the World of Men. This palace was built of shiny, white, smooth stones that gleamed in the light. And, while it had as many towers as other castles, these were topped not with battlements but with roundish structures, something like onions with their pointed bits jutting upward. Most of all, there were no walls around the outside.

"Ridiculous," Galahad said. "Who could defend a castle like that?"

"Maybe it wasn't built to be defended," Ellyn said tartly. "I think it's gorgeous."

They rode down a long slope toward the shining castle, and as they rode they came to a statue, carved from the same smooth white stone as the palace itself. Beaufils stopped to admire the figure, of an armored knight in a heroic pose. Galahad gave the figure a scornful glance as he rode by. "Do they imagine that a stone warrior will help them in a war?" he asked with a faint sneer.

Beaufils prodded Clover into a walk to keep up with the others, but he glanced back over his shoulder one more time at the statue. The sight made him gasp, because from this side, the statue looked very different: now the noble knight was a scowling destroyer, his eyes alive with bloodlust and his sword dripping with gore. "Ellyn?" Beaufils said softly, but the others were already too far ahead to hear. Giving the image one more look, Beaufils turned and hurried on.

As he caught up with the others, they were just coming to a second statue. This one was of a majestic, smiling queen who was holding out a hand filled with food for her grateful people. As they rode past, though, Beaufils turned to look at the statue from the other side. Again the figure was different in reverse. Now she was a pale and evil-looking woman with her people cringing at her feet. Only the crown on her head was the same.

And so it went. They passed a magnificent king who, from the other side, was a shriveled hunchback counting piles of money. There were two young men, brothers or close friends, who from one side were embracing each other and from the other were driving daggers into each other's backs. There was a loving mother, surrounded by her adoring children, whose opposite aspect was of a lumpy lady troll with her children in chains at her feet. A tall man holding an armful of parchments and wearing robes like those worn by Clerk Geoffrey back at Camelot was on one side teaching a youth and on the other sneering at the world from behind a pile of books. Last of all, just before they came to the great front door of the palace, was a glorious angel whose other aspect was that of a goat-footed demon. Neither of Beaufils's companions looked over their shoulders to see the altered images, and Beaufils said nothing, but as they came to the palace, he guessed that whatever they found there would likewise not be what it seemed.

The door swung open and a majestic man in gleaming black clothes stood at the threshold. "Welcome, travelers," he said, sweeping a low, courtly bow.

"We greet you, sir," said Galahad. "Are you the master of this castle?"

"I am."

Ellyn frowned. "Isn't this the castle of Lady Synadona?"

The man's smile faded slightly, and he bowed to Ellyn. "Yes," he said. "I was about to explain that. I am her ladyship's vizier, caring for her interests until she is able to do so herself."

"Oh?" Beaufils asked. "Is something wrong with Lady Synadona?"

"Regrettably, yes," the man replied. "She is gravely ill. So ill, in fact, that she is unable to receive guests. But I will be happy to serve as your host and give you lodging on your journey."

Galahad bowed his head. "We are grateful to you, sir," he said.

Ellyn shook her head. "No, that won't do."

The man raised his eyebrows haughtily. "Won't do?" he repeated.

"We were told to see Lady Synadona herself," Ellyn said.

"May I ask who told you this?"

Ellyn hesitated, then said, "An anchoress named Irena. She said that we might be able to help the Lady Synadona."

The man smiled and shook his head sadly. "An anchoress? And what could a recluse know about the real world?" he said. "I assure you, young lady, that everything possible is being done for Lady Synadona. I, and I alone, have managed to keep her alive by my own magical arts."

"Magic!" Galahad exclaimed, his hand dropping to his sword.

"Yes," the man said. "I am called the Necromancer, and I am an enchanter of great skill. By my spells and potions and every other hidden art, I have succeeded in prolonging the Lady Synadona's life. But I will not have my science meddled with. You may not see her ladyship."

"But how could a visit hurt?" Beaufils asked mildly.

"You do not understand," the Necromancer said.

"I understand this, though," Galahad said suddenly, leaping from his horse, his sword in his grasp. "I am sworn to oppose magic and all the forces of evil!" With that, he plunged toward the door where the Necromancer stood, except that the magician was no longer there. He had disappeared in a roiling ball of green smoke that came rushing out the doorway. Without hesitation, Galahad threw himself into the smoke and disappeared.

"He *is* brave," Beaufils said to Ellyn. "You have to give him that much." Ellyn only stared, so Beaufils dismounted and took her hand. "Come on," he said. "Galahad may need help."

They walked into the castle through the already thinning smoke, and found themselves in a grand hall with corridors leading off in every direction, like the threads of a spider's web branching away from the center. The hall itself was empty.

"Now which way?" Ellyn asked.

"Don't ask me," Beaufils replied. "You're supposed to lead, aren't you?"

"Oh, bother. That's right," Ellyn said. "Very well. This way." Still holding Beaufils's hand, she led him down one of the passages. "What am I looking for?" she asked.

Beaufils grinned. "Isn't that what Terence told you to figure out?"

"Very funny," Ellyn said. "If you don't know either, just say so. All right, I think Galahad can take care of himself, so I'm looking for Lady Synadona. I don't know what's wrong with her, but I'll wager that Necromancer fellow is the problem, not the remedy. Let's go left here."

For several minutes she picked her way through a maze of halls, past dozens of doors. When she came to a choice of directions, she never hesitated but just chose a path and pressed on. Before long they heard the unmistakable sound of swordplay, and a minute later they came to an open area before a large door, where Galahad was locked in combat with two knights. To one side the Necromancer stood, wringing his hands and shouting, "Kill him! Kill him!"

But this clearly was beyond the knights' ability. Beaufils watched in awe as his friend fought with uncanny skill. Galahad was truly a wizard with a sword. He made no unnecessary move, was always in exactly the right place, and in another minute had disarmed both knights. They turned and fled down a hall. The Necromancer, meanwhile, had reached into his robe and drawn out a long, polished stick. Stepping behind

Galahad, he raised the stick above his head. Beaufils didn't know what was going to happen, but he saw that Galahad was not watching, so he leaped between Galahad and the Necromancer—just as a glimmer of green light sprang from the tip of the stick toward him. Beaufils saw, but didn't feel, the beam of light hit him in the chest, then bounce away. "What was that?" he asked the Necromancer.

The Necromancer's eyes widened with fear, and he shrieked, "No!" Then, to Beaufils's considerable surprise, he picked up his long robes and scampered off down a corridor.

"Beau, are you all right?" shouted Ellyn.

"I think so," he replied.

"Didn't you feel anything? That magician just cast a spell on you."

Beaufils shrugged. "Not much of a spell." He turned to Galahad. "Well done, Galahad! I've never seen such skill."

"Much as I hate to say it," Ellyn said, "Beau is right. That was brilliant swordplay, Sir Galahad. Come on, then. Let's see what these knights were guarding." Striding briskly forward, she pushed open the door at the end of the anteroom and stepped in.

Following her, Beaufils entered a warm and cozy room, lit with the orange glow of a large fire and many branches of candles. There was a bed against the wall, with no one in it, and a plush chair by the fire, but it too was empty. Ellyn was also looking about the bare room. She caught Beaufils's eye and said, "I was sure we'd find her here."

Before Beaufils could reply, a soft female voice came from behind the direction of the chair. "Who are you?"

Then, as Beaufils and Ellyn watched in speechless awe, a long, scaly head appeared over the arm of the chair. Inch by inch, the head was followed by a long serpentine neck, which coiled up from the floor by the fire and wound itself around the chair. The creature's scales glinted in the firelight, orange and shimmery green and glossy black. Then, as the snakelike body rose higher, two knobby feet appeared, gripping the arm of the chair and pulling the body up to its full height.

"A dragon. It's a dragon," said Ellyn.

"Oh, is that what a dragon looks like?" Beaufils asked. "How lovely they are!"

"Saint George be my help!" came a shaky voice behind them. It was Galahad.

"Who are you?" the voice said again, and Beaufils saw the dragon's lips move. He hadn't known that dragons could talk, but then he looked into the creature's eyes and he was no longer surprised. They glowed with lively intelligence and a great, aching sadness.

Ellyn was also gazing into the dragon's eyes, and her face suddenly filled with sympathy. She stepped forward nervously. "Please, ma'am," she said. "My name is Ellyn. Can you help us find Lady Synadona?"

The dragon nodded her head slowly. "I am she."

"You? But you're a . . . I mean . . . have you always been . . . ?"

"No," Lady Synadona said. "I was once a woman like you."

"Did that Necromancer fellow do this to you?" Ellyn asked indignantly.

The dragon shook her head. "Not really. Yes, he performed the spell, but at my request. It was why I brought him here. I wanted power. I wanted people to fear me. And now I can barely face what I have become."

"Can you . . . I mean, is there any way that you could be . . ."

"Restored? Yes, there is one hope, but it will never happen."

"What is the one hope?" Beaufils asked.

Lady Synadona bowed her head. "There is, in a different world, a great king named Arthur, who is surrounded by great knights. The spell over me can only be broken if I am kissed by the son of Arthur's greatest knight."

Beaufils smiled broadly. "Lady Synadona, I have some good news for you." He gestured at Galahad. "Allow me to introduce Sir Galahad. Galahad is the son of Sir Lancelot, who everyone says is Arthur's greatest knight."

Ellyn's mouth dropped open, and her eyes began to shine. She looked beseechingly at Galahad. "Sir Galahad," she said. "This *must* be why we've been sent here."

Galahad's face twisted in an expression of disgust. "You want me to kiss that thing?" he asked.

Ellyn looked steadily at him. "Yes, please, Sir Galahad." Then, after a brief pause, she knelt on the floor. "I beg you, sir, to do this. Kiss this dragon and rescue Lady Synadona."

Galahad stared at Ellyn, and for a second he hesitated, but then his face grew hard again. "No," he said harshly. A humorless smile spread over his face as he shifted his gaze to the dragon. "You were clever, but I know who you are now."

The dragon looked sad, but she only said, "I have not lied to you, sir. I am no more than I said I was."

"You are that same fateful serpent who seduced our mother Eve and thus brought evil upon mankind! Now you seek to lure me also into temptation." Galahad raised his sword. "Stand back, Beaufils. I shall rid us of the Temptress forever."

"No!" shouted Ellen, but Galahad had already leaped forward, his arm striking out with blinding speed.

Beaufils, moving just as quickly, caught Galahad's arm but was only able to check the blow partially, and the sword bit into the dragon's neck. Bright red blood spurted from the wound, and the dragon made a low moaning sound. Galahad snatched his arm from his companion's grasp and with a heavy blow cuffed Beaufils across the face, knocking him down. From the floor, Beaufils watched with horror as Galahad raised his sword for another blow, but then Galahad froze. Ellyn had thrown herself over the dragon, shielding her from Galahad's second strike.

"Very well, Lady Ellyn!" Galahad declared, lowering his sword. "The monster will die soon anyway. I have now at last defeated her. I have destroyed the Temptress!" With a cry of triumph, he rushed from the room.

"After him, Beau!" Ellyn shouted. "Bring him back. He must kiss her! I'll try to stop the bleeding."

Beaufils nodded and ran from the room, chasing the echoes of Galahad's receding footsteps. He dashed for what seemed forever, but was probably only a few minutes, through the web of corridors, coming out into the great entrance hall just in time to see Galahad dive through the door. Beaufils sprang after him, plunging over the threshold and throwing himself onto Galahad's running form. They both went sprawling in the dust outside the palace.

"Stop, Galahad!" Beaufils said. "You have to come back! Lady Synadona needs—"

He got no further. His words were drowned out by a deafening crash and rumble, louder than a clap of thunder, followed by a thick cloud of dust. Beaufils released Galahad and looked about in wonder, but he could see nothing in the storm of dust that swirled about. At last the air cleared, and before Beaufils's stricken eyes appeared a peaceful meadow by a river, and nothing else. Lady Synadona's castle was gone.

XI

CARBONEK

"What have you done?" Beaufils shouted furiously at Galahad.

"I've done it! I've done it!" Galahad crowed joyously. "All my life I've struggled with temptation, but now I have seen sin in its true form and have defeated it!"

"And what if we've lost Ellyn too?" Beaufils shouted, tears of anger and grief welling from his eyes.

"At last I have been made worthy!" Galahad shouted, ignoring him. "Now surely I will achieve the Holy Grail!"

"And *what about Ellyn?*" Beaufils screamed.

At last Galahad seemed to hear what Beaufils was saying, and he shrugged. "Don't you see? She too was part of my temptation. Surely you saw how beautiful she was. She also had to be driven away."

Beaufils's jaw dropped. Fury welled up inside him. "She was not part of your temptation, blast you, Galahad! She was a person!"

"And look! Just as I expected! The boat has come to take me to my goal." Galahad jumped to his feet and began running toward the river where a great wooden boat lay up against the bank.

"No!" Beaufils shouted, scrambling to his own feet. "Come back!" He raced after Galahad, but the knight had too great a lead, and Beaufils didn't catch up to him until he was already on the boat. Beaufils threw himself aboard and grabbed hold of Galahad, but a sudden jerk made him lose his grip. The boat was moving. Beaufils ran to the rail, but by the time he got there, the boat had left the shore and plunged into a dense fog. He couldn't even see the water, let alone the riverbank and the place where the palace had stood. There was nothing to do but let the boat take them where it would. Galahad moved to the front, his eyes bright with anticipation, while Beaufils sank to the wooden floor and wept.

Beaufils could not have told how long he and Galahad rode through the cloud, with no sound but the lapping of water along the sides of the boat. It could have been hours or days or just minutes, but eventually they came out of the mist to a bright sea before a towering island fortress. Beaufils felt his heaviness lift slightly as they emerged from the fog, as if he were either waking from a dream or just beginning one, and then the boat crunched up onto the gravel beach of the island.

"Come, Beaufils," commanded Galahad. He leaped lightly from the boat, and, having nowhere else to go, Beaufils followed him. A path led up a long rocky crag to the fortress door, and they climbed the path together, neither speaking until they came to the castle itself. "This must be it, the home of the Holy Grail," Galahad said breathlessly.

The door swung outward noiselessly, revealing a long line of old men standing just inside the castle, in a neat row, as if they had been waiting. "Yes, Sir Galahad," said the oldest of the men, who stood at the center of the line. "This is the Castle Carbonek, where resides the Holy Grail. You are welcome."

Galahad sank to his knees, uttering a prayer of gratitude, but Beaufils remained standing, staring at the row of men. There were ten of them, their faces all very old but their bodies and their posture as straight and strong as those of young men. Several of the men were dressed in armor of different types and held swords. Others wore long dark robes like Clerk Geoffrey and the Necromancer, and still others wore outfits like Bishop Baldwin's garments. The man who had spoken wore a long cape of some lush purple material trimmed with fur, and on his head was a golden crown.

"Rise, Sir Galahad," said the crowned man. "You

and your squire have been deemed worthy to join us at Carbonek. You and you alone have achieved the Quest of the Holy Grail. I am King Josephus, the son of Joseph of Arimathea, and I have been waiting hundreds upon hundreds of years for this moment, the moment when our number shall at last be complete. It was for this moment that we sent the chair and the sword to Camelot on the day before you arrived: to call you to this place."

"You've been here hundreds of years?" Beaufils repeated, raising one eyebrow.

"We are kept alive by the Grail," King Josephus said. "But you will see. Come join our feast."

As one, the ten elders turned and walked in two lines, keeping in strict order, down a great hall. Galahad fell into place at the end of one line, so Beaufils went to the other. The procession made its stately way down the hall and into a vast banquet room, where the ten elders took seats on either side of a long table, still in order. Thus Beaufils ended up at the last chair on the left side of the table and Galahad at the very end, looking all the way up the long board to the other side, where King Josephus sat on a throne that looked even more uncomfortable than King Arthur's jeweled seat. Beaufils wondered that, in all those hundreds of years, it had never occurred to King Josephus that another chair might be more pleasant to sit in, but he said nothing.

The long banquet table was empty, but as soon as all were seated, King Josephus clapped his hands, and a door opened at the end of the hall. Through the opening, floating like goose down on the breeze, came the Grail itself. It was the same large golden platter that had appeared at King Arthur's court, and just as had happened then, a plate of food appeared before each of the elders and Galahad and Beaufils. The Grail went to the center of the table, then stopped, and floated there, immobile.

Wordlessly, the elders turned to their plates and began to eat, so Beaufils followed their example, politely eating from the plate of fresh fruit and vegetables and brown bread that had appeared before him. It tasted very good.

When the silent meal was done, the plates disappeared and were replaced with twelve small goblets. The Grail began to move again, floating above until it was directly before King Josephus. The king rose to his feet and, taking his goblet, dipped a swallow of some liquid from the lip of the Grail and drank it. At once he seemed to grow stronger and more youthful. Then the Grail moved to the next man at King Josephus's right, who followed the king's example, then across the table to the man at the king's left. One by one, in this zigzag pattern, the Grail went to each of the elders, who each drank a swallow from the clear liquid in the Grail. At about the seventh elder, Beaufils decided not to wait any longer. "Excuse me, King Josephus, but what exactly is this Grail?"

The Grail stopped, and all the elders turned their ancient eyes toward Beaufils. King Josephus held up his hand, as if to calm them, and said, "Peace, friends. Galahad's squire is young and innocent—indeed, we know that he is innocent, or he could not have come here. He does not understand." Then he looked at Beaufils. "You do not know it yet, in your youth, but you will learn it. Here at the Castle Carbonek, all that need be known is known already. There is no need to ask questions."

"But what if you want to learn something?"

At this second question, the king's brows drew together, but only for a moment. At last he said, "You disturb our order, child. All you need to know will be made known."

The Grail resumed its procession back and forth across the table until all ten elders had been served. Then it came to a place directly between Galahad and Beaufils and stopped.

King Josephus said, "Take and drink, my children, for you are the last two men to be deemed pure enough to join us. For these many years we have been waiting until the day that we would become the Twelve Guardians of the Grail. The Grail gives us food and restores our life. In this place we have lives without end, without distress, without toil. You may join us."

Galahad seemed too overwhelmed to speak, but Beaufils had to ask one more question. "Sir," he said, "why are there no women in this place?"

"Drink," King Josephus said, his voice stronger but still calm. "Drink, and all your questions will cease."

Beaufils frowned. "Yes, but will that be because I'll know the answers or because I won't have any more questions? I mean, there's a difference."

King Josephus sighed heavily. "As you say," he replied. "I will answer this question alone. The drink that is in the Grail is from the miraculous spring that the ancient pagans called Lethe. Anyone who drinks from those waters will be swallowed forever in the peace of forgetfulness. You will be protected from every temptation, from now unto eternity. You will recall no grief, no pain, no sin. You will feel no lust or covetous-ness or pride. All the trials, the passions, and the toils of that distant world called the World of Men will fade away forever. You will remember no person or object that could distract your thoughts from the peaceful contemplation of eternity."

"I have dreamed of this day," Galahad said suddenly. "I have dreamed of such peaceful waters."

Beaufils looked into his friend's face and then, in a

moment of insight, at last understood. Behind Galahad's eyes he saw clouds of fear and realized that it had always been fear that had driven his friend. Galahad was brave in battle but terrified of the world, which to him would always be an evil force trying to destroy him. In his fear, Galahad could never rest, never relax, and never trust. To Galahad, the waters of Lethe represented release from fear.

"Drink, my son," said King Josephus.

"Yes," Beaufils said. "Have a drink, my friend."

Galahad took up the goblet from his place and scraped it across the bottom of the Grail, scooping up a few drops of the liquid. He raised the cup feverishly to his lips and drained it. Then, as Beaufils watched, Galahad's expression changed. The suspicion that had always lurked behind his eyes faded and was replaced by pure bliss. His face no longer showed any doubt, fear, or even recognition—only an overwhelming contentment. Galahad let out a long sigh and relaxed into his chair.

"And now, my child," King Josephus said to Beaufils. "It is your turn."

Beaufils shook his head slowly and said, "No."

Beaufils stumbled across the barren wasteland, his mouth parched and his whole body crying out for water.

He wasn't sure if this was part of his punishment, but he had a feeling that King Josephus would approve of it anyway: dying of thirst would be an appropriate penalty for refusing to drink from the Grail.

The king's stern words upon Beaufils's refusal of the Grail still reverberated in his mind. King Josephus had spoken in a calm voice—evidently he'd been telling the truth when he said that the waters of Lethe took away all passions—but there had been no kindness in his speech either. "Then begone from this island, and from this place of peace forever, you child of wickedness. Few are offered this grace, and none have ever refused it. No one who has beheld so great a salvation and then turned away can be restored. Child of wickedness I called you, and so you are. You are no longer fit to remain on these shores."

Beaufils had barely had time to look at Galahad and note the mild and disinterested expression on his friend's face before the banquet hall began to fill with clouds before his eyes. In a blink he found himself back on the pilotless ship, rushing away through the fog, and seconds later the boat had emptied him onto a bleak shore.

That had been early morning, judging from the sun. It was now nearly sundown, and Beaufils had been walking all day. He had had nothing to drink and, but for a crust of bread that he'd found in his pocket, nothing to eat. He had set off to find the place where Lady

Synadona's castle had disappeared, where he hoped to find Ellyn, but the boat from Carbonek had left him at a different place on the shore, far from any river, and now Beaufils was hopelessly lost.

He sank into the long shadow of a craggy boulder, to rest for just a moment from the heat. He knew he would die soon without water. A faint skittering sound at his feet made him open his eyes, and he saw a long-legged mouse standing by his leg, examining him with interest. "Hello, dear," Beaufils said. His voice was harsh and raspy. Leaning to one side, Beaufils dug in the pocket where he had found the crust of bread and managed to produce a few crumbs. "Here you go," he whispered, holding them out to the mouse.

"Isn't that all you have?" said a low voice from beside him—a woman's voice.

Beaufils turned and looked into the eyes of the most beautiful woman he had ever seen. It wasn't that she was beautiful in appearance—he still didn't understand that idea exactly—but she was beautiful in goodness and humor and love. "It will do me no good," he explained through his cracked lips. "But it will be a whole meal for the little one."

"Yes," the woman said, smiling. "Just like the pool of water behind that hill. I don't especially need a drink, but you look as if you could use one."

Beaufils could only stare, and so the woman took his

arm, raised him to his feet, and led him to a blissfully cool pool of water, from which a stream ran gently through the parched earth. "Who are you?" he gasped to the woman when he had had his fill.

"My name is Lorie," the woman replied. "I am the daughter of an old friend of yours, Ganscotter the Enchanter."

"Scotus?" Beaufils asked.

"The same. He sent me to help you."

"That was nice of him," Beaufils murmured. Then a memory stirred him to say, "But he isn't always nice, is he?"

"What do you mean?"

"Well, he cast that spell over Ellyn's father—the Carl of Carlisle, and also over the Lady Petunia. He changed them into horrible creatures."

"My father can do things that no human or faerie has ever dreamed of doing," Lorie said. "But even he cannot change someone into something they don't want to be."

The idea was familiar. "That's what Lady Synadona said too, about when she became a dragon." He looked up suddenly. "Please, Lorie, can you tell me if she is all right? And my friend Ellyn?"

"I cannot say," Lorie replied. "All I can tell you is where to seek them yourself. Follow this stream. In a few miles it will bring you to a field, and beyond that a forest. In the forest you will find helpers to take you the rest of the way."

"Helpers?"

"My brother and a friend," Lorie said. "I know you are tired, but you should leave now, before it grows dark."

An hour later, having followed the stream to the forest, Beaufils staggered into a small clearing, where he had seen the flickering of a fire, and collapsed. He heard an exclamation of surprise, a sword being drawn, then a voice saying, "Wait!"

Summoning his last strength, Beaufils rolled over and looked up into the old-young eyes of the squire Terence. Beside him was Beaufils's old friend Gawain.

XII

Transformations

The next few minutes were a flurry of activity, as Terence and Gawain gave Beaufils food and water and checked him for injuries. At last, after Beaufils had assured them for the twentieth time that he would be all right soon, Gawain asked earnestly, "Where's Ellyn?"

"I'm looking for her now," Beaufils said.

Gawain's face grew tight. "You've lost her? But that hermit, Basil, promised me that she would be all right in your—"

"Why don't you tell us what happened, Beaufils?" Terence interrupted.

So Beaufils told about the past days, from their crossing into the World of Faeries and meeting Galahad to Ellyn's decision at Lady Petunia's castle, up to when they found Lady Synadona, then lost her again, along with Ellyn. "Now I'm trying to get back to the meadow where the castle disappeared, to find them," he concluded.

"But hang on," Gawain said. "Where's Galahad?"

"We've separated," Beaufils replied.

"That much my powerful intellect had surmised," Gawain said. "But why? Why isn't he helping you look for Ellyn?"

Beaufils thought for a moment. He didn't want to criticize Galahad, which made answering tricky. "He had his own quest, I guess."

"What quest was more important than Ellyn?" Gawain demanded indignantly.

"He went after the Grail, you see."

Gawain rolled his eyes. "That Grail again. I know I won't ever find it, but I'm beginning to wonder if anyone will."

"Actually," Beaufils said, almost apologetically, "we did."

They both stared at him blankly. "You found the Grail?" Terence asked.

Beaufils nodded. "Yes, after Lady Synadona's castle disappeared. I chased Galahad onto a boat, which took us to an island castle where ten old men met us and showed us the Grail. They fed us a very nice banquet, then invited us to drink from the Grail and stay forever. Galahad drank."

"And you didn't," Terence said.

"I couldn't. I had to find Ellyn." Then he added, "But I'm sure the Grail is a wonderful thing. When Galahad drank, he seemed happier than I'd ever seen him, so I can't say *he* made the wrong choice. It's just that I couldn't do it."

Gawain looked thoughtful, but Terence gave Beaufils a warm smile. "We'll find her," he said. "In this world, you always find what you really seek. Maybe in every world. Do you know where to look?"

"Lady Synadona's castle was by a river," Beaufils said. "Do you think if we followed this stream it would lead us to her?"

"We'll leave in the morning," Terence said.

Gawain looked sharply at his squire. "Terence, we can't go with Le Beau."

"He needs our help," Terence replied. "He's alone and on foot."

"Yes, I see that," Gawain said. "But we have to get our information to Arthur."

Terence only shrugged, and Beaufils asked, "What information?"

Gawain replied, "I told you once, didn't I, why Terence wasn't at Camelot when you first came? He had gone to ask his father about some rumors of rebellion. Terence's father, I ought to explain, is a man of some knowledge."

"Yes," Beaufils said. "Ganscotter the Enchanter. I know."

Terence looked surprised. "You know my father?"

"I met him back in the World of Men," Beaufils replied. "But there he called himself Scotus."

"Then you understand why I went to him," Terence said. "He sees things that the rest of us don't. I couldn't find him at first—perhaps he was back in the World of Men meeting you—but I finally caught up with him. Even then he wouldn't tell me anything until I had done a chore for him."

"What chore?" asked Beaufils.

Terence grinned. "Can't you guess?"

"Oh, yes," Beaufils said, nodding suddenly. "He sent you to help Ellyn and me make the crossing to this world, didn't he?"

"That's right. He has some particular interest in you, Beaufils. Anyway, after I'd done that for him and gone back, he told me that there really is a plot."

"Against King Arthur?"

"Yes," Terence said. "Not a revolt or a battle, at least not at first. Father says this plot will work from the inside, by corrupting and dividing the Round Table itself."

"I can't see it, myself," Gawain commented. "We're all loyal to the king."

"Father says the plot will come through a young man

whose heart is so filled with hate that it's like a stone. He couldn't tell us who this young man is, though."

Beaufils let his breath out slowly. "Mordred," he said. Gawain and Terence looked at each other, then back at Beaufils, who explained, "The young man's name is Mordred. I recognize him from your father's description."

Gawain eyed Beaufils speculatively. "You know, Le Beau, you're a curious case. Just a few weeks ago you came out of the woods as innocent and ignorant as a kitten, but now . . . I can't help feeling that you, like Ganscotter, see things I never will."

Beaufils shrugged. "I don't know about that, but I *have* seen a lot." He smiled reminiscently. "The first man I ever met, before I left home, told me I should stay in the forest because I would only find wickedness in the world. Well, I *have* found wickedness—greater and deeper wickedness than I ever imagined. I've even been to the place of death. But it hasn't all been so bad. I've also seen people like you two and the hermits and Bors and Galahad, people who set their face against the Evil and try to stand against it." He hesitated, then added, "Sometimes they try in really stupid ways, mind you, but the trying counts for something."

Terence touched Gawain's arm. "We can tell Arthur about this Mordred soon enough. First we'll help Beaufils."

They set off shortly after dawn, with Beaufils riding behind Terence. Gawain apologized for this arrangement. "You really ought to ride behind me. My Guingalet is stronger and can hold two better than Terence's mare. Unfortunately, he's getting short-tempered in his old age and won't carry a second rider."

"Oh, yes," Terence murmured. "Poor horsie's not sweet-tempered and gentle, like he used to be."

"Your horse is named Guingalet?" Beaufils asked.

"It's an old Orkney name," Gawain said. "Half my ancestors have names that start with Guin-, so it makes him almost part of the family."

Beaufils was conscious of a wistful stirring within. This huge black horse with the baleful eyes had a name and a family, while he himself still had neither. But he only said, "Shall we go?"

Gawain scouted ahead on Guingalet while Terence held his mare to a moderate pace, conserving her strength. "I suppose your mule is at Lady Synadona's castle, too?" he asked.

Beaufils nodded. "I hope so. We left our animals by the front door when we went inside." After a few minutes, Beaufils asked, "Tell me about *your* family, Terence."

Terence smiled. "To say truth, you and I have a lot in common. Like you, I grew up not knowing my father— or mother, for that matter. She died when I was a baby. I was raised in a hermitage in the World of Men by a holy man named Trevisant. I didn't find my father was until I was about your age."

"What about your sister?"

Terence turned in his saddle and stared at Beaufils. "You know my sister?"

Beaufils nodded. "Lorie helped me find you last night."

Terence whistled softly. "Father really does have an interest in you, Beaufils. What did you think of Lorie?"

"I loved her," Beaufils replied simply. "She's what beauty ought to mean—all goodness."

Terence nodded at the distant figure ahead of them that was Gawain. "I know one who would agree with you. Gawain is Lorie's husband."

Beaufils blinked. "What?"

"I won't tell the whole story, but they met some fifteen or sixteen years ago. Gawain was a brash young knight, eager to prove himself by winning tournaments and battles, and just as eager to prove himself with the ladies, I might add. Then Lorie came to court and called us on a quest that changed us both. That was when I found my family, and Gawain found a love to be faithful to. They were wed a few years later, but they've lived in their different worlds ever since, both waiting for the day when they can be together forever."

"When will that be?"

"I don't know. Father says that Gawain has more to

do in the World of Men. We don't know what, but it has to do with Arthur." Terence smiled at Beaufils over his shoulder. "It's hard on Gawain, but you understand," he said. "You also turned your back on a world in order to help a friend."

At that moment, Gawain, who had been riding ahead of them, topped a hill, then stopped abruptly. Wheeling his horse, he galloped back toward them.

"This must be it," he called when he was near. "A huge marble palace with cupolas on towers and statues all around."

Beaufils nodded, and Terence booted his mare into a gallop. They rode together up the hill, and looked down on Lady Synadona's castle. Beaufils could even see Clover and the horses, quietly grazing by the river. He slipped down from behind Terence. "Let's go."

The others dismounted and followed him down the hill, along the avenue of the two-sided statues. As before, when they came to the front door, it swung open as if by itself, but this time the figure that stood across the threshold was no towering magician in long robes but a rather shriveled old man swathed in a black garment much too big for him. "Go away," he wheezed at them. "No visitors on weekends."

Beaufils's mouth dropped open as he stared into the old man's face. It was changed, but there could be no mistaking it. This was the Necromancer.

The Necromancer recognized Beaufils too. "You!" he shrieked suddenly. "Get out of here! Go away, I say!"

"I can't," Beaufils replied. "I've come for Lady Ellyn. But don't worry. I don't mean you any harm."

"Be quiet!" the old man snapped, covering his ears with his hands. "Don't say that!"

Beaufils was puzzled. "Say what? That I don't mean you any—?"

"Shut up! Shut up!"

"But why?"

The withered figure scowled at Beaufils. "It's a lie, that's why! How can you say you mean me no harm? Look at the harm you've done me! You did this! You did this!"

"*I* made you like that?" Beaufils asked, bewildered. "But how? I really didn't mean to—"

"Will you shut up about that? Just rubbing it in, you are! Oh, I know your type. You've come to gloat over me, haven't you?"

"I don't understand," Beaufils said. He couldn't help feeling sorry for the shriveled specimen before him.

"Don't understand, do you? Well, let me explain it, if it will give you so much pleasure, you loathsome insect! I was once the greatest enchanter in all the world."

"Which world?" Beaufils asked. "Because in this world there's Ganscotter the—"

"Will you please shut up?" the old man snapped. "I

238

was the *greatest*, I tell you, and the reason I was the greatest was because by my own arts I had discovered the most fearsome power dreamed of! All dominion was mine, and I was about to take it, too. I would have been the most powerful ruler in all the world, but then you came along! Why did you have to come here, anyway?"

"It was nothing personal," Beaufils protested.

The Necromancer began to hop up and down, screaming, "I said to shut up about that!"

"Why don't you want me to say anything nice to you?" Beaufils asked.

"That's the whole problem! Don't you understand, you pock-bottomed toad? That's what you did to me! The power I had gained—at great personal sacrifice, I might add—was to use other people's fear and hatred against them! All I had to do was wave my wand at someone, and all the fear and hate that he felt for me would turn right back on him! It was perfect, because everybody hated me! So I bounced their hate right back at them, and it destroyed them! It was foolproof!"

The Necromancer was almost raving now, and flecks of foam had appeared at the corners of his mouth. Hoping to calm him, Beaufils said soothingly, "That certainly *was* very clever of you, sir."

"Don't patronize me! Shut up, shut up, shut up! You're just trying to make it worse than you already have!"

"But what did *I* do?"

"Don't you remember? I cast my spell on you, right after your friend had beaten my guards, and *it bounced away!*"

"Yes, I remember that, except that I didn't know what spell you were casting. Why did it bounce off, anyway?"

"Because-the-spell-would-only-work-on-people-who-hated-me, you looby!"

"But I don't hate you."

The Necromancer turned purple and couldn't speak for a moment, and when he did, his voice was shaking with passion. "I'm well aware of that, thank you! And because you didn't hate me, all my work, the work of a lifetime, has been destroyed! My power began slipping at that moment! Within a day after you left, even my invisibility curse faded and the castle reappeared."

Beaufils nodded with comprehension. "Ah, now I see," he said.

"I know you see!" the man squealed. *"Didn't I just say that? Didn't I?"*

"Yes, you did," Beaufils said. "I'm sorry."

"And don't apologize either!"

Beaufils took a breath and glanced over his shoulder at Gawain and Terence, both of whom were grinning broadly. He let his breath out and said, "Look, it's very sad that you lost all your powers, but as I said, I really didn't come to see you at all. I want to see Lady Ellyn and Lady Synadona."

"You didn't come to see me?" Beaufils shook his head, and the Necromancer's eyes began to bulge. "You destroy the greatest enchanter of all time, and you don't even care to see what you've done?"

"No," Beaufils said. "But look, if there's anything I can do to help you—"

"Nooo!" the man shrieked. "It needed only that! You want to *help* me, do you? How cruel can a person be? You . . . you're *despicable!*"

With that, the Necromancer turned and stalked away, taking up a broom from beside the door. As Beaufils led Gawain and Terence into the great entry chamber, he was vaguely aware of the old man half-heartedly sweeping the flagstones behind him.

Following the same route that Ellyn had chosen on their earlier visit, Beaufils led his friends through the maze of corridors to Lady Synadona's chamber and pushed open the door. There, in the armchair by the fire, sat Ellyn, with the gleaming, serpentine body of Lady Synadona coiled about her. As the door opened, Ellyn looked up quickly. "Beau!" she said, her tone a mixture of relief and anger. "Whatever has taken you so long?"

Beaufils stepped into the room. "Galahad didn't want to come back," Beaufils said apologetically.

"How did you convince him?" Ellyn asked. Beaufils only shook his head. "Beau, you *did* bring Galahad back, didn't you?"

"No, Ellyn."

"Oh, Beau!" Ellyn said, her eyes filling with tears. "Now what are we to do? Synadona's dying! I've done everything I can think of, but the wound Galahad gave her won't heal."

Terence and Gawain stepped into the room behind Beaufils and stopped, both staring at the scene before them.

"Gawain? Squire Terence?" Ellyn said bemusedly.

"I ran into them on my way here," Beaufils explained.

"That's the dragon you told us about?" Gawain whispered. Beaufils nodded, and Gawain said, "Are you sure it was telling the truth about being a woman under a spell? I mean, you don't hear about many honest dragons."

Ellyn shook her head, one tear rolling down her cheek. "No, Gawain, it isn't like that. She's really who she says, and she . . . before she grew too weak we were able to talk and . . . oh, until now I'd never met someone who needed me but wouldn't use me . . . Squire Terence, you were the one who told me I should find out what my quest was. Well, I've found it—it's to find someone I care about, someone I would give myself for willingly and freely. And now—" Ellyn's face crumpled up and she began to sob softly. "Now I've failed."

Terence said quietly, "Tell me again what Galahad was supposed to do."

"Kiss her. She can only be restored to her true shape by a kiss from the son of King Arthur's greatest knight." Ellyn looked at the squire hopelessly. "Squire Terence, who is your father?"

"Not one of Arthur's knights, if that's what you mean," Terence said.

Ellyn turned her eyes toward Gawain, but he shook his head. "My father was a knight, all right, but not one of Arthur's. In fact, my father died fighting Arthur."

Beaufils stepped forward and took Ellyn's hand in his. "Ellyn," he said. "There may be other ways to help her. I've a feeling that there are always more ways than we know." He knelt beside Ellyn and reached down to where Lady Synadona's reptilian head lay in her lap. "My lady," he said. "I don't know who my father is, but I want to help you." Then he bowed his head and touched his lips to the dragon's rough face in a gentle kiss.

A dazzling light exploded from Lady Synadona, and Beaufils lurched backward and sat down hard as Ellyn gave a yelp of surprise. At first Beaufils thought that Lady Synadona had burst into flame, but although the blaze of whiteness blinded him, he was not burned. Everything went black, then red, then shaded with rainbow hues. Beaufils wasn't sure if the colors were really in the room or if they were just his eyes trying to readjust to dimness after that brilliant glare. It was nearly a minute before he could see clearly again, but when he could, he became aware of a woman kneeling beside him. She had long auburn hair, was wearing only a thin and ragged shift, and her eyes were fixed on Ellyn.

"Synadona?" Ellyn whispered.

"Ellyn," the woman said. "You saved me."

Ellyn looked dazed, but she managed to shake her head. "No, Beau saved you."

The woman turned and looked at Beaufils, her eyes solemn. "Thank you, sir, for restoring me. But Ellyn stayed with me and saved my life."

Then Ellyn began to cry, her face a curious blend of happiness and disbelief and exhaustion and something else that was stronger. Beaufils felt suddenly like an intruder, and he rose to his feet. "Lady Synadona," he said, "I am glad I could help. Now I think that my friends and I will leave you for a moment. You'll, ah, want to change clothes."

Lady Synadona looked down at her shift, then smiled. "I suppose I should be glad that the spell left me any clothes at all. Will you come back in an hour, so I can thank you properly?"

Beaufils, Terence, and Gawain agreed and left the chamber. "It seems you were right, Le Beau," Gawain said. "The kiss didn't have to be from the son of Arthur's greatest knight, after all."

"Maybe," Terence said.

Now that Ellyn had been found and Lady Synadona restored, Gawain and Terence were eager to return to the World of Men with their message for King Arthur. To no one's surprise, Ellyn had decided to stay behind, Lady Synadona's new chief lady-in-waiting and best friend. "It's not one of those Castles of Women you told me about," she said to Terence, "but it's where I belong. At last I've found a person who would love me if I were ugly—and a person I would die for. If you see my parents, will you tell them I'm well?" Gawain promised he would make a special trip to Carlisle as soon as he was able. "And Beau?" Ellyn asked. "Will you come visit me?"

"As often as I can," Beaufils replied, smiling. Then the three men rode away, down the avenue of statues. Beaufils noticed with mild interest that none of them changed appearance as they passed. They weren't all pleasant figures—some of them had assumed their evil side as their permanent form—but they were now all plainly one thing.

"How do we get to the World of Men?" Beaufils asked once they were away.

Gawain only glanced at Terence, who replied, "Well, that's a bit tricky, actually. There aren't any permanent gateways. Sometimes I know exactly where a passage is and how to get there, but that's generally only when I'm helping someone else make the crossing, like when I helped you and Ellyn that day. Other times I recognize a crossing when I see it. Still other times I need help myself."

Beaufils stared at Terence. "Then we have no idea which way to go?"

Gawain grinned. "It's not quite so bad as that. The crossing is nearly always through water, so we can stay by this river."

"In the meantime," Terence added, "watch out for old friends. You never know who'll lend a hand."

Beaufils tried be watchful, as Terence had suggested, but he found it difficult. As the day went on, he grew more and more distracted, his thoughts turning inward to his own situation. It had occurred to him suddenly that he had nowhere to go. Ellyn had finished her quest. Galahad had achieved the Grail. Even Sir Bors had completed a quest of sorts, having conquered his own guilt. Gawain and Terence had discovered news that was important to King Arthur, so they had a purpose. But what of him? What was his quest? He had helped everyone else achieve their quests, but he himself had achieved nothing. He hadn't even found out who his father was, the whole reason he had left home to start with. They trotted down a small slope, and as Clover jumped a stone, one of the bags on the mule's back thumped against Beaufils's leg. He glanced at the bag, then snorted softly as he realized what had hit him: the black river stone he had found on his first day away from home. It was still in the bag with his other "treasures": the bird's nest and the long white feather. Beaufils shook his head sadly. Childish things. How could he have come so far since setting out, and changed so much, only to arrive nowhere at all?

They made camp that night by a mountain brook, still looking for a crossing to the World of Men. Gawain was starting to fret at the delay, but Terence remained calm. "We'll get back, milord," he said. "Do you imagine that worrying will make it happen faster?"

Gawain grumbled something about "uppity squires" who were most annoying when they were right, then rolled up in his blankets by the fire. A few minutes later, Terence followed his lead, and before long Beaufils could hear from them both the even breathing of sleep. He moved back from the fire and sat against a tree at the edge of the darkness.

"You've been thoughtful today, Beaufils."

Beaufils smiled with relief but didn't turn his head to look. He now realized he'd been waiting all day for Scotus to appear. "I was wondering about my quest," he said.

A stirring at his right told him that Scotus had sat beside him. "And what quest would that be?" Scotus asked.

"That's the problem, sir. Everyone else seems to know their quest, and then they achieve it. I keep remembering how Terence told Ellyn that she first needed to find out what her quest was, and as soon as she did, it was over. But I don't even know what I'm looking for."

"Yes," Scotus said. "Terence was right when he said that to Lady Ellyn. Some people need to know their goal or they can't search at all. For others, though, the quest itself is enough." Beaufils puzzled over this, and then Scotus said, "But I thought you *did* know your quest. Weren't you trying to find out who your father is?"

Beaufils sighed. "Yes," he said. "I was. But I've forgotten why. It doesn't seem very important just now."

"Would you like me to tell you?"

Startled, Beaufils at last looked at his friend. Scotus sat in utter stillness beside him, his eyes—which were equally still—watching Beaufils with affection. "Who my father is?" Beaufils asked. "You mean you know?"

"I've always known," the old man replied.

Beaufils stared at Scotus. All the wistfulness he had felt just that morning returned, his envy of how Gawain and Terence and even Gawain's horse Guingalet had families. But the wistfulness faded quickly. Even if he did know who his father was, what would he do? Try to become a part of his father's life? Once he had thought so, but now he knew that he didn't want just to be a part

248

of someone else's life and goals, even his own father's. He wanted his own quest. He shook his head, hesitantly at first, then more firmly. "I guess not," he replied. "As I said, it doesn't seem very important today."

Scotus nodded. He didn't seem surprised at all.

Beaufils said, "Did you already know what I would say?"

"No one knows for certain what someone else will choose."

"Not even an enchanter?"

Scotus smiled. "Not even an enchanter. So you know who I am?"

"Except for your real name. Is it Scotus or Ganscotter?"

"When you travel to worlds other than your own, it doesn't matter much what name you are called," Scotus replied. "In the World of Faeries, I'm Ganscotter. In the World of Men I have at least a dozen names."

Beaufils frowned suddenly. "Now there's something that I *would* like to know."

"What's that?"

"My name. Mother called me Beaufils and Sir Kai, Le Beau Desconus. Gawain calls me Le Beau, and Ellyn, just Beau. Oughtn't I to have one name that is just me and not be someone different with every new person?"

"Indeed you should. Why don't you choose one?"

"I *could* do that, I suppose," Beaufils admitted. "But

didn't my mother have a real name for me before she fell into the habit of calling me just Beaufils?"

Scotus nodded. "She did." He was silent for a moment, then said, "You should know your mother's story. Her real name was Yvette, and she was the daughter of a respectable and very moral nobleman. I suppose your mother found her upbringing a bit stifling, because she left home at fifteen to become a lady-in-waiting at Camelot, dallied with a young knight, and, as a result, conceived you. Ashamed, she returned to her home, but her father turned her away. That was when she went to the forest, bore you into this world, and made a new home. A courageous woman, your mother."

For the first time in his life, it occurred to Beaufils to wonder how his mother had survived. He couldn't imagine any of the noble ladies he had met since leaving home being able to live alone in a forest. He looked questioningly at Scotus.

"Yes, my boy. I helped her. I admire courage, and I saw great potential in her baby."

"So," Beaufils asked, "what did she name me?"

"Your name is Guinglain. She meant to tell you, I think, but in her final illness, she didn't think of it."

"Guinglain," he repeated softly. "Yes, I think I can make something of that."

"You already have, my boy." Scotus stood. "Shall I

come visit you the next time I am here in the World of Men?"

"Please do," he replied. "You know what name to ask for." Then he realized what Scotus had just said. "What do you mean, *here in the World of Men?*"

"You've been back in your own world since I sat beside you. Somewhere near the town of Leeds, I believe. You can tell Gawain and Terence when they awake." Then he stepped into the darkness and was gone.

"When the deuce did it get so cold?" said Gawain, rolling out of his blankets the next morning. "It's as if we went from midsummer to late fall overnight."

Beaufils, or Guinglain—as he meant to think of himself now—huddled in his blankets and glanced up at him from the fire. "Tell me, Gawain. When you travel from one world to another, do you ever find yourself in a different time as well?"

Terence, who had been loading their horses, turned quickly to look at Guinglain. Gawain replied, "Ay, lad. Sometimes."

"What do you mean, Beaufils?" Terence asked.

"Well, we're in the World of Men again," Guinglain said.

"When did this happen?" Gawain asked.

"While you were sleeping."

"Do you have any idea where we are?" Terence inquired.

"Near some town called Leeds."

"Yorkshire," Gawain said. "We'll have several days' ride yet. Pity we couldn't have made the crossing to a more convenient spot."

Terence replied with only a soft, noncommittal murmur. His eyes were on Guinglain. "You had a visitor last night?"

Guinglain nodded, and Terence asked no more questions. They ate breakfast by the fire, then mounted and rode away. Terence and Gawain both had warm clothes, but Guinglain still wore his old sleeveless leather jerkin, so he kept his blankets wrapped around him as they made their way south through the chilly, damp wind. His feet grew numb by midday, and the rest of him never got warm, since the blankets kept slipping from his shoulders. A nice warm cloak or a few minutes out of the wind would be nice, he reflected.

At that moment, as if in answer to Guinglain's wish, they came upon a small, deserted house in a weedy clearing. The hut had the dark windows and forlorn aspect that mark every deserted house, but it looked to be in fair condition, and there was an unfinished woodpile behind it. Gawain halted in the yard. "Shall we stop here for a bit? We can eat inside, out of the wind."

"Is anyone home?" Terence wondered aloud.

Guinglain looked about the forest clearing, his brow furrowed. Then he smiled. "No one will be home," he said. "This is a hermitage, but the hermit has left."

"You've been here before?" Terence asked.

Guinglain nodded. "Yes. With Ellyn, Sir Bors, and Sir Lionel."

"And you're sure the hermit's gone?" Gawain asked, dismounting.

"Pretty sure," Guinglain replied. "He didn't really seem cut out for the holy life."

Gawain said, "Well, if there's no one here, let's find a place for the animals and go inside."

Another memory came to Guinglain, and he leaped from Clover's back. "There's something else he doesn't need now," he said, running into the house. There it was, still hanging where he had left it: the thick, warm robe the hermit had thrown down before leaving. Guinglain pulled it over his head, glad that this particular hermit had not chosen to wear the rough, bristly haircloth that some other holy men used. Gawain stepped into the room, followed by Terence. Gawain blinked at Guinglain's robe.

"Do you like it?" Guinglain asked. "It's very warm."

"You look like a holy man," Gawain said, distaste in his voice.

"I think it suits you very well," Terence said. "Shall we eat?" He produced some food from their gear, but before they could begin on it, they were interrupted by a loud knock. The door swung open to reveal a tall, broad-shouldered woman in peasant's clothes, who was holding a sturdy, glowering boy by the hand. "Hello?" she called out in a grating voice.

"Hello," Guinglain replied.

"Good! They told me in t'village that there wasn't no hermit anymore, but I came to see for meself, them bein' all knocks-in-the-cradles. I needed a holy man, you see."

"You've come to see the hermit?" Guinglain said.

"Ay, I've come to see you."

"Me? But . . . I . . ."

"I know you're not t'same hermit as was here before, which is a pity, because he was a right one, but you'll do." At that, the woman jerked the boy's arm, nearly lifting him from his feet. The boy clamped his jaw shut and glowered at the ground. "It's this bewitched son of mine!" she snapped. "He won't mind me at all! Don't seem to matter how hard I beat him, either. He's a child of wickedness is what he is, so I brought him to you! Do ye think he has a devil?"

Guinglain looked at the boy's sullen face, and his heart grew strangely warm. "I'll speak to him, mistress," he said gravely. "And see if I find a devil in him." From the corner of his eye, he saw Gawain and Terence blinking at him, but he only smiled. Stepping forward,

254

he took the boy's hand firmly from his mother's and led him briskly outside. As soon as the door was closed, he released the boy's hand. "Sorry if I was rough," he said. "I thought I needed to be firm, or your mother wouldn't have let go. What's your name?"

"Bert," the boy muttered.

"Well, Bert, why don't you come with me over behind those trees?"

"What're ye going to do?"

"Get out of the wind. I wonder if there's a stream back there. There has to be some water around somewhere. Come and help me look."

They went together into the woods until they found a brook spilling into a small pool. Guinglain dipped his face into the pool and drank. Bert just watched him.

"Are ye going to beat me?" he asked suddenly.

"Much good *that* would do," Guinglain said with a laugh. "I'll wager you can take any beating, and without crying at that."

"Well, I can, too," Bert said belligerently. "But the other hermit whipped me when Momma brought me to him."

"And look what good it did," Guinglain said mildly. He shook his head and added, "I couldn't punish you anyway. You know how your mother called you a 'child of wickedness'?"

"She's always calling me that."

"Well, I'm one too."

"What?" Bert looked up, his eyes wide.

Guinglain nodded. "God's truth. Not three days ago I was in a great castle, and an old king held out his hand and told me so. 'Child of wickedness'—those very words! So how could *I* punish you?"

"How can a holy man be a child of wickedness?" Bert asked suspiciously.

"Well, the thing is, I don't *try* to be wicked. It just happens, I guess. So I keep trying to do better, and maybe that's enough for a beginner. The hermit who used to beat you, he must have been just about perfect himself or he couldn't have done that, but I'm not like him. I'm more like you."

"You're like me?"

"Just like you. I don't try to do *wrong*, exactly, but I don't like obeying commands that I think are stupid or wrong, so I end up making people mad at me. I guess you and I are children of wickedness together."

Bert stared at Guinglain, speechless.

Guinglain grinned at him. "There ought to be a guild for people like us. You know, the Noble Order of Children of Wickedness, or something like that. There might even be a few more of us about."

Bert thought this over. "My sister Gussie's pretty wicked."

Guinglain nodded. "Yes, this would have to be a

guild for both boys and girls. And it wouldn't just be common folks like us. I know an earl's daughter named Ellyn who could show us all a thing or two."

"A guild!" Bert said excitedly. "And we can use your hermitage as our guild hall!"

Guinglain felt a sudden stab of remorse, as he realized that Bert had taken his banter—meant only to reassure the boy—more seriously than he had intended. "Well, Bert, it's not really my hermitage, you know," he said.

"But you *will* stay, won't you?" Bert asked, his eyes bright. "The other hermit's gone. And we could have meetings, and even a treasury."

This took Guinglain by surprise. "Treasury? But I don't have any—"

"I do!" Bert said triumphantly. He jammed his grubby fist into his shirt and produced a shiny gray blob. "This is a lump of real iron that Smithy in t'village let me have. If you hold it right, it looks just like Father Gerald from the church. See? This shiny bit's the top of his head."

Guinglain began to laugh. It was as if a bubble had suddenly burst inside, and a light, airy joy had been released, filling him from his toes to his ears. He laughed so hard that tears came to his eyes, and for some time he couldn't speak. Bert stood his ground, but he watched Guinglain's paroxysm nervously. At last, though,

Guinglain was able to reply. "Yes, Bert. I'm staying," he said. "And I have some treasures, too. I have a white feather as long as your arm, a bird's nest, and a really great black stone." Bert looked impressed, and Guinglain took a deep breath, savoring the cold air. "Come on then, Bert," he said. "We should go back to your mother."

As they stepped into the hermitage, Guinglain grasped Bert's arm roughly. Bert met his eye, then nodded and assumed such a woefully contrite expression that Guinglain had to struggle not to burst into laughter again. "Ma'am," Guinglain said briskly. "I've spoken to your boy here. He is a stubborn case, but I think he may do better now."

"He'd better," the woman said.

"I don't promise that he's healed, mind you," Guinglain added. "You may very well have to bring him to me again."

Bert's mother nodded with satisfaction. "You'll give him a taste of what he deserves, then?"

"Exactly what I intend, ma'am," Guinglain said, with all the sternness he could muster.

Bert's mother took her son by his other arm and marched him out of the hermitage. Guinglain called over her shoulder, "I hope you've learned something today, Bert!"

"I have, sir!" the boy replied earnestly, but when his mother wasn't looking, he looked back and gave his new friend a private smile.

Guinglain stood in the doorway watching the two cross the unkempt clearing. He became aware that Terence was at his side. "You're staying, then?" he asked, but it wasn't really a question.

"I've a fancy to become a holy man," Guinglain replied.

"You're mad," Gawain said, joining them.

"Yes," Guinglain replied. "That should help, don't you think?"

Just then Bert's mother stopped and turned back toward them. "Pardon me, but I don't know your name, sir. The others in the village ought to know we've a new hermit, but I don't know what name to tell them."

Guinglain nodded. "Tell them that I'm Brother Guinglain."

"Brother Guinglain," the woman repeated. Then she turned back and continued away.

"Guinglain?" asked Gawain, his voice strained. "Where did that name come from?"

Guinglain looked at his friend curiously. "I picked it up on my quest," he replied. "I thought I'd see what I could make of it. Why? Don't you like it?"

Gawain shook his head dazedly. "It's not that," he

said. "It's just that . . . it's my grandfather's name, a good man. I always used to say that if I ever had a son myself, I would call him that."

Then Beaufils understood, and looking into Gawain's eyes saw the same revelation dawning there. For a long moment, father and son grinned wordlessly at each other. At last, Terence broke the silence.

"Now I see why Father has shown so much interest in you," he said. "And you're still going to stay here? Are you now done with all your questing?"

Guinglain chuckled. "Oh no. I think everything I've done up to this point has been preparation. I'm just now ready to start."

Half an hour later, Gawain and Terence took a fond farewell of Guinglain, promising to be back soon. Then the knight and the squire rode back to the king's court, and the holy man went to sit by the fire in stillness and begin his quest. He didn't exactly know what he was looking for, but he knew what to call it: the Fair Unknown.

Author's Note

At the height of the Middle Ages, if you were a poet or storyteller, then the chances were that you wrote about King Arthur and his court. It was just what you did. Medieval bards who wanted to tell adventure tales told about Arthurian knights on quests, slaying dragons and defeating recreant knights. The ones who preferred love stories told about Arthur's knights and their ladies. Some of the stories were masterpieces, and some were very bad, but they all took place in King Arthur's court.

Sometimes, even people who didn't want to tell stories at all latched onto the Arthurian world. At any rate, this seems to have happened in an anonymous French book called the *Queste del Saint Graal*—The Quest of the Holy Grail. The author of this book—most people think he was a thirteenth-century monk—wasn't really interested in Arthur or his knights. He just used them as scenery for his real purpose: to describe the spiritual quest for God. This the *Queste* does with allegories and symbolic dream interpretations by the cartload, a lot of inaccurate but imaginative history, and, distressingly often, with sermons. You can hardly read a page without encountering one of the holy hermits who lurk behind every other tree and getting yet another sermon proclaimed at you.

For his spiritual allegory, the author of the *Queste* wanted an irreproachable hero, but since all of Arthur's celebrated knights were known to have broken at least one of the Commandments (generally the same one), he had to invent his own: Galahad. This hero is such a vessel of virtue that we have to admire him, or at least *ought* to. It *is* hard to like the fellow, though. So when I took up the story of the *Queste*, I imported my own hero, an innocent fellow named Beaufils, from a cheerful, rambling Middle English romance called *Lybeau Desconus*, which means something like "the Fair Unknown."

In this book, then, I've woven together several different stories. The parts about Galahad and Bors all came from the *Queste*, although some of Bors's adventures were originally about other characters, and the episodes that focus on Beaufils, Ellyn, Lady Synadona, and the Necromancer are all from *Lybeau*. I even tossed in one extra story, a brief English romance about Sir Gawain called "The Carl of Carlisle." No particular reason; I just like the story.

Starting out with a monastic allegory has made this book a bit different from my earlier Arthurian retellings, but it has also given me a chance to show another side of my chosen time period. The Middle Ages was a profoundly, and sometimes oppressively, religious time. There really were hermits and monasteries and priests and little churches scattered about everywhere; there really were anchoresses (such as the wonderful Julian of Norwich) who shut themselves in tiny cells, finding joy in their solitude. In my earlier books, I've had heroes who were squires, ladies, pages, minstrels, knights, and fools, and to be fair to the medieval world, I really needed a religious hero too. And, while my holy man might not have passed muster at a real thirteenth-century monastery, the *Queste* itself encourages those who start this journey to make their own path.

That evening they considered how best they might proceed, and agreed to separate the following day and go their several ways, for it would redound to their shame if they rode in a band together . . . Then they rode out from the castle and separated as they

*had decided amongst themselves, striking out into the
forest one here, one there, wherever they saw it thickest and wherever path or track was absent.*

Queste del Saint Graal

—Gerald Morris